HEARTS CURSED

GODS CURSED SERIES BOOK 4

LEISL LEIGHTON

Published by Leisl Leighton as Permien Press. For more information, email: leisl@leislleighton.com

First published 2022 in the A Perfectly Paranormal Christmas Anthology.

Cover design – Samantha Marshall; Editor – Marnie St Clair

eBook ISBN: 978-1-922836-16-8; Print ISBN: 978-1-922836-17-5

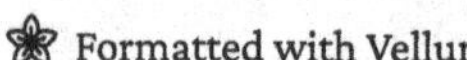 Formatted with Vellum

PRAISE FOR THE GODS CURSED SERIES

Was really hard to put this one down once I started! I can not wait to see what this new series ... Gods Cursed Series.... Holds in the future!

— DIANA K – GOODREADS & BOOKSPROUT

Loved this and it's Easter orientated. Check this out.

— WHITNEY – GOODREADS AND BOOKSPROUT REVIEWER

"So good! I will always love paranormal romances, they just have so many different types, and themes, and never get boring. Leighton delivers a great one!"

— TAPNCHICA – GOODREADS AND BOOKSPROUT REVIEWER

I absolutely love this ... Leighton brilliantly weaves in Greek and Nordic Mythology, Oestra/Easter themes, and a HUGE splash of her rich and thrilling imagination. She is a master at world building, character, plot, and oh...those sex scenes are pretty damn hot. You'd be crazy not to read this series!

— LAURA BADHUS – GOODREADS REVIEWER

Loved it !! love this series !! love Korinna and Tamuel.. this is their story... they have history... a fast paced fated mates , second chances, cursed drama... a fast paced action packed drama... so good!!!

— KIMKIM – GOODREADS AND BOOKSPROUT REVIEWER

This was magical and captivating throughout. Thoroughly enjoyed the storyline and characters and how they overcome things.

— PAT'S REVIEWS - GOODREADS REVIEWER

I loved this! ... I loved reading about the history and what happened to set things in motion. This is a very good book and is most definitely worth reading.

— A SCHOFIELD - GOODREADS & BOOKBUB REVIEWER

HEARTS CURSED

PROLOGUE
DEMETER'S SACRIFICE

"I do not wish to do this, my beloved boy."

Triptolemus' gaze met Demeter's, steady and sure as ever. "You must, D. You know it is the only way."

"But I do not wish to lose you," she said, hating the quaver in her voice. If it was anyone but he, she would smite them for witnessing her weakness.

"I will still be here."

"But you will not be you. And you will not know me. You will know nothing."

"I will know this." He gestured to the snow-laden pine forest around them, his expression peaceful.

To her, in this moment, the prettiness of the green frosted branches of the conical-shaped trees wasn't peaceful at all. It was a slap in the face given the ugliness of what she must do with the spell they'd crafted.

He sighed, turned back to her and said, "My need to do my work will remain. It will be enough."

"Will it?"

"It must be." He swallowed hard, stood tall, chin raised,

vibrant green eyes full of all the love and life and giving that was so much a part of him. A part of him she was about to steal away. "Do you think I wish to leave my beloved when I know my disappearance will hurt her beyond endurance? To leave before my daughter is born, to never know her, not until such a time she is strong enough to utilise her powers and endure the burden of foreseeing in a way even Cassandra could not?"

He took a deep breath, but not soon enough to cover the throb of grief in his voice; a throb she wished she could take away but couldn't. Not for him; not for her; not for any of them. Because he was right.

They had to do this.

He continued calmly when most would fall prey to their emotions – including her. "I wish I could stay. I wish this burden was not ours. But you cannot unsee what you saw. And I cannot allow myself, or my daughter because of me, to be used by one of the Old Titans for such ill purposes." He took a shuddering breath, shoulders straightening further so he looked like one of Ares' soldiers. "Promise me you will make sure my beloved does not suffer."

"I promise."

"And promise me you will look after my daughter like she is yours."

"Persephone will take her as one of her Soteira. She will want for nothing. And we will ensure she is hidden for as long as we can."

He nodded, then looked away over the snow-tipped pine trees surrounding them, before, fists clenched at his side, he said, "Do it now, before I change my mind."

She lifted her hand to start the spell, but hesitated. Instead of touching the edges of her magic, she reached out to touch his handsome face, to glory in the spring green of his eyes – a green that represented his ties to her and Persephone and Gaia, and marked him for this fate.

They'd tried everything to change the path of destiny that led to the future she'd seen. But the tri-power that had been mixed with a strange other-power – a power she was certain had come from the Eternal Well itself – that had caused his miraculous creation, marked him and his offspring in a way that made them targets for a mad Titan and his rage, and nothing could undo what had been done. All they could do was postpone what was to come until the players were ready – well, as ready as they could be.

She sighed, her hand dropping to her side. "I vow, with all the love for you I have in my heart, that I will find some way of bringing you back to us before you lose it all."

His eyes widened. "No! I do not ask that of—"

But the Eternal Well had already heard her vow, the rolling knocks in the distance cutting off his protest.

Tears filled his eyes. "What have you done?"

"What must be done to ensure a happy ending." The rolling knocks were a sign that the Eternal Well had accepted her vow, had written it into the Halls of Power and tied her existence to its fulfillment.

"But there is no happy ending if you die."

She smiled softly as she cupped his face one more time. "My dearest boy, the son of my heart if not my body, have some faith in me."

Then, because she could stand the torture of this goodbye no longer, she cast the spell they'd created, taking everything from him that made him who he was except the power in his veins and the immortality that would forever mark him as different from all humans on this Earth he so loved; or most Gods for that matter.

It was a difference that would see him wander, a lost

soul, never able to settle in one place for long, never to belong, eternally hearts cursed and lonely because of a cursed prophecy.

It was the only thing that would keep him safe. The only thing that would keep his daughter safe until she was ready.

The spell made him jerk and clench his teeth, frothing at the mouth for interminable minutes until, finally – thankfully – he passed out.

She caught him, cushioning his fall, laying him in the cold snow under a large pine tree next to the bags of coin that would help him in his new life. After making certain he was safe under the shielding branches and wouldn't be covered in the snow now falling from the sky, she turned and opened a portal to her home.

She stepped through and immediately knelt down beside the pond of foreseeing she'd had Cassandra make for her before the other woman's constant visions had driven her insane. Until Korinna was born and grew old enough to handle the power of foresight that would be hers, someone among the pantheons must still be able to see and understand and try to stop the danger that was coming for them. Not that anyone but she, Persephone and Triptolemus believed in what she'd seen.

Her brothers and sisters and all their children were nothing if not consistent in their belief that they were untouchable. As far as Zeus and Hades and the others were concerned, they had defeated the Titans once, and were certain they could do it again even if one of them did make it past the Void that separated the Beyond from all the Realms. The Gods and Goddesses of other pantheons were no better in their egotism.

They relied too heavily on Cassandra and the Fates.

Idiots, all of them!

They went on and on about the hubris of humanity, but honestly, hubris, thy name be ... insert any name of any God or Goddess that ever was or ever would be!

They were concerned only with their power and how to hold on to it.

So short-sighted.

But she wasn't. She had seen the future and couldn't deny it.

She waved her hand over the waters of the pond, looking, searching to see if her actions today had created the change they desired.

The dark future was still there, but it was fogged, parts of it flickering and changing over and over as the echoes of her actions affected the ripples of time.

She waved her hands and part of the vision cleared to show her the birth of a boy-child, not long after Triptolemus' baby girl was to be born, whose life seemed twined with hers. She would need to dabble in that boy-child's life and the life of his parents to ensure a favourable outcome.

She sighed. So much to do.

She hoped it wouldn't be too little too late. She wished she could talk to her Triptolemus. He always made her feel better. Her chin wobbled. "Please, Eternal Well, don't let the sacrifice I made, that my beloved boy made, be in vain."

There was no sign her plea had been heard, but then, that wasn't really the way the Eternal Well worked. Still, she wouldn't stop praying to it. Even a Goddess as powerful as she needed to pray to something.

Roping her thoughts back in, she stared at the ripples before her.

There was a face in the water now. A woman's face. The image glowed strangely — first blood-red, like the gem she'd wrested from Tiberinus a century ago, then changing to the colours of dawn, before being washed in blood-red then finally settling on shining silver, like moonlight. There was something familiar about it. Something she ...

She gasped. Could this be the soul trapped in the HeartsBlood Gem? Is that why she'd been so determined to take it? She'd never quite known what to do with it, having no interest in the prophecy that tied the soul inside the gem to God Killer powers. She'd put it with the rest of her collection of powerful gems and trinkets. But she should have known it meant something. The Eternal Well could move in mysterious ways. Was it trying to tell her something about the gem or the soul inside?

As if in answer to her question, the ripples from that image bled out and linked with the ones of Triptolemus' fate. Which could only mean one thing:

The soul in the gem and her precious Triptolemus were linked in some way!

How, she didn't yet know, but it was something when she'd had nothing before. Something that might help her fulfill her vow despite the unfortunate prophecy. Now, she just had to figure out how she could use it to her advantage while bypassing that particular prophecy.

She had no plans to die now or in the future.

She had to see this war with the oncoming darkness that was Perses through to its conclusion. A conclusion she would force to go her way, even if she had to sacrifice her heart.

CHAPTER

ONE

Ilia sat bolt upright, hands clutching at her chest. Her heart thundered under her ribs – so hard, so fast – it felt like it might tear itself in two.

"Fuck-fuck," she gasped, blinking sweat from her eyes – or was it tears?

Both. "Fuck."

Her chest was hot. She looked down to see glowing pinkish-gold light. It had to be Clodia, the evil ancient witch now trapped in the HeartsBlood Gem she'd melded into her chest months ago.

But how could the bitch-witch be doing this? It had taken Ilia centuries of being trapped inside the gem to figure out how it worked, and centuries more to be able to affect the person wearing it. There was no way the evil old witch could have discovered those secrets so quickly and used them against her.

So what the fuck was this?

"Wait a minute." The gem usually glowed red, not pinkish-gold. Maybe this wasn't Clodia. Maybe this had something to do with her newly acquired powers.

She still knew so little about them. Her own powers had been burned out after fighting Clodia in the Void. She wasn't unhappy about that given they were part of the reason she'd been blood-cursed into the gem in the first place – even though they'd not been strong, they had been perfect to mesh her soul with the gem. She would have been perfectly happy never to have powers again, but no, of course she wasn't allowed that kind of peace. These ones had been 'gifted' to her when Tamuel's use of an ancient spell from the Eleusinian Mysteries Grimoire and Dawn's burgeoning powers, so incredibly strong even though she'd just been born, had given Ilia a corporeal form.

It still made her shudder that part of that spell had used blood magic. Blood magic had been what locked her inside the HeartsBlood Gem all those years ago. Why hadn't she realised that all those times Tamuel had used the sigil spell that it used blood magic? He'd carved it into his skin for fuck's sake! At the time she'd put it down to the fact that there were many spells that only worked if made a part of the worker in some way. She'd thought that the blood was just a by-product of the carving not that it was powering anything.

But when he'd used it on her – as it had always been meant to be used, to make a worthy spirit corporeal – she'd realised just how important the blood was in the working of the spell. She'd been so shocked – and it had happened so quickly – she'd not been able to stop him. Then after, she'd been so overwhelmed by the new life she'd been given, and the fact that everything she'd lost was once again a fresh wound in her now corporeal heart, she'd barely been able to say anything.

After they'd got home and she'd come to terms with what had happened, it had seemed churlish to make a fuss when Tamuel's intent had only been good. As had Korinna's use of blood magic with the Eleusinian Mysteries Grimoire and the ring she'd got from her long-lost father. Although, from what they'd been learning, that had more to do with the qualities of their blood being magical. So it wasn't really blood magic in the way she knew – and hated – it. It was something else entirely.

But blood magic – it wasn't good. Look what it had done in this instance: tied her to the baby whose magic had been instrumental in letting her live again and in getting them out of the Void.

Thinking of it made the power in her chest flare brighter.

Fuck. She put her hand to it, feeling its warmth, its urgency. She couldn't go out there like this. The others would worry – and they already worried enough.

She had to think of something else.

The dream. Yes. Her dream. She needed to try to remember it. It had felt important.

She closed her eyes, breathing slowly, bringing the feeling she'd woken with back to the fore.

Fragments of her dream fluttered to life, but stayed foggy and elusive. All she could grasp was that it had been a thing of import – a great hope and a terrible loss.

She gasped, eyes snapping open. The dream must have been about her sons. They were the only thing that had ever made her feel this way. That everything inside her had shattered.

But why could she not remember?

She hissed a sound of frustration. She wanted to remember. Her memories of her sons, in the brief moment she had with them before they were torn from her because of some stupid prophecy, were all she had of them.

That and the fact she had failed them by trusting in the wrong God.

After both Mars and her uncle's betrayals, she had stupidly trusted Tiberinus when he said he could help her find her sons. Desperation, innocence and gullibility had worked together to make her agree to give her blood to the River God. He said he would use it to help track down the She-Wolf who had taken her sons after her uncle had ordered them – and her – killed because some idiot had intoned a prophecy about them that made them a threat to his rule. Instead, Tiberinus had drunk of her freely-given blood to sever her soul from her body and used her magics to tie it to the powerful gem he was desperate to use, but couldn't without a living soul inside it – a soul that must be hers, he'd told her, because of where her power originated from and the prophecy that tied her to Beings of import.

At the time, she'd assumed he meant the prophecy about her sons, but she'd later come to realise it was another one about someone known as the God Killers. Somehow she was tied into that prophecy, although she still had no idea why. Given the tiny amount of magic she had in the scheme of things – and the fact that her power was most useful for healing – she wasn't a threat to anyone, let alone a God.

She wished it was. It would make revenge so much easier if she could kill a God.

Of course, the fact she was nowhere near powerful enough to kill a God hadn't mattered to the Fates or Tiberinus, and she'd been trapped inside the HeartsBlood Gem for thousands of years. Her one hope had been that, one day, she'd come into the possession of Tamuel and Korinna, the two lovers who, according to what she'd overheard

Demeter and Persephone say when she was in Demeter's possession, were the key to her freedom.

She snorted. Some freedom. It, like everything else in her life, had come with a catch. In this case, a baby-sized one and the tether that tied them together.

She supposed it could be worse. She could be tied to some arsehole God. At least this way, she was tied to gorgeous little baby Dawn, who she'd come to love. Even though every moment spent with her was like a stab in the heart because it reminded her of how little time she'd spent with her boys.

Remembering them was a joy, but also a terrible, unbearable pain. Pain she clung to with everything in her despite the fact that her failure to find them and stop their bleak future from playing out, one killing the other in the name of power, plagued her sleep.

She lifted a shaking hand and roughly swiped at the sweat on her brows, the tears that wet her cheeks and dribbled off her chin. "Enough sitting here thinking about a past that cannot be changed," she said into the silence of her room. "I've got work to do and a future to plan."

An image of a man – the man she kept dreaming about – swept across her mind. Her heart throbbed with a knowing – a recent addition to her new powers, one she wished had been 'gifted' to someone else because of how nebulous and unhelpful they could be.

Take this knowing for instance. It told her that somehow this man in her dreams could heal her of her pain. How, or why or even when wasn't part of the knowing. Just a certainty she couldn't explain.

Or trust.

No male had ever brought good into her life. Only betrayal and darkness and hate.

Tamuel brought goodness into your life. And his father, Bastien, is a good man too. They would never betray or cause harm to those they love, especially their mates.

She grunted at the thought her subconscious threw up. So, there were a few good men in all the Realms. It really wasn't likely there was another. Certainly not one that would pass her way to help her. And certainly not one who she could ever trust enough to help heal her deepest pain.

She blinked, her lip curling at the stupidity of such a romantic thought. The only person who could heal her pain was herself. And she didn't want to. Because if she did, she might lose the very thing that kept her going day after day – her need to find those responsible for all that had happened to her so she could make them pay.

It had been so satisfying taking down Clodia and trapping her in this gem. She wanted to experience that feeling again.

The thought made her heart thunder; the glow in her chest brightened.

Damn it!

Taking herself in hand, she breathed deeply, slowly until finally – finally – her heart stopped thundering and the glow in her chest faded.

Now the only glow was the one that the sunrise – shining its rays through her bedroom window – gave to her skin. Thankfully, the dawn light that had glowed from within her after her 'birth' had ceased doing so months ago. It had been awkward leaving Stevens' House radiating like a sunrise. But then, that was the price you paid when an ex-Cupid and a powerful newborn baby witch used an ancient forbidden spell and their magic to shove the power of Ostara, Goddess of Dawn (among other things), into you to turn you from a spirit into a living, breathing being with a power that was as mysterious as it was unstable. Well, maybe not unstable. But it wasn't something she could easily control.

She was trying to learn though. Because even though she didn't want the power, uncontrolled powers were dangerous. Not just because they could lash out at others, but because they could be used by others against you. And she was never going to allow anyone to have that kind of control over her ever again.

Speaking of learning, she better get on with her day, because Korinna and Tamuel would need more leads to follow to try to find Triptolemus. Despite that she'd shared what she'd overheard when in Demeter's possession about the fact that Triptolemus, an ancient God – or demi-God; they really weren't certain – was Korinna's father and that he'd been stripped of his memories and hidden from all the Gods in all the pantheons because of some danger to him or Korinna or both, they still knew so little. Every lead she'd found had turned up nothing more than a confusion of myths and legends that didn't lead to where he was now or how they might get his memory back.

Korinna was handling it well, but Ilia knew the other witch was upset over their lack of progress. Not to mention, the thing that had escaped from the Void at Easter was still out there and, while they guessed it had something to do with the danger they faced, they knew precious little else. It hadn't made itself known to them yet – but it would, and when it did, they needed to be ready.

The only way they could be was if they found Triptolemus and helped him gain his memories back. What she'd overheard Demeter say had been clear on that at least.

Typical, the Goddess hadn't said anything more helpful

they could really use to track him down. But then, when was the last time a God or Goddess had ever been helpful? There was always the chance this Triptolemus would be as unhelpful for whatever Godly – or demi-Godly – reasons he had. Although, given this danger had something to do with him – or Korinna, or both – he was far more likely to fill them in than Demeter or her daughter.

She sighed.

So, aside from her lessons, there was a lot more research to get on with today. Not to mention, she still hadn't found anything useful about how to break her connection with Dawn. Except of course, the entry in the grimoire she'd read months ago that suggested blood magic would do it – that under certain circumstances, it would create a stronger bond with someone else that would snap and supplement the life-force bond she shared with Dawn. What those circumstances were, it didn't say. Not that she would ever consider using it. Who knew what more it might do to that precious little baby? Blood magic always asked for a price.

She shook her head to dispel the unpleasantness and threw the covers back. She needed a hot shower and a nice hot shot of espresso and then she could get on with her day.

TWO

Trip swiped at the sweat on his brow for the fifth time in as many minutes, then dug the fork into the soil. He had to get this field finished. It was more important than he could explain. Not that he was trying to explain the urgency that had taken over him. It was just something he had to do. Now. Today.

Sweat stung his eyes and his t-shirt was clinging to his back, but he ignored both. He couldn't stop. Had to keep going.

The handle of the fork slipped in his hands. He stopped long enough to wipe first one then the other on his jeans, ignoring the slight sting. It didn't matter. Nothing mattered but getting this field finished.

More sweat stung his eyes, too much to ignore. He lifted his shirt and rubbed it over his face. As he lowered the shirt, his gaze caught on his watch.

Shit! It was well after lunch. Daphne should be back by now with the emptied trailer so they could do another load before she left to pick up her youngest son. Where was she? He had more than a full load for her. Not that it was enough. The flooding river had dumped so much rubbish into the field.

Why the fuck had the flooding rains come now? And right after the hail that had ruined his orchard, stripping it of fruit and leaves. It was perfectly biblical. What was next? A plague of locusts?

No. He wouldn't let any of this ruin his appreciation of the season.

Christmas.

Just the thought of the coming season made him smile.

He loved Christmas. Learning about Christmas and helping to spread the joy was the second bright light he'd had after waking to this memory-less existence, with only the bags of gold left beside him and the clothes he wore as clues to who he might have been. He'd long ago stopped trying to push past the pain that came every time he endeavoured to remember – a pain so terrible, he'd inevitably pass out. Trying to remember only led to frustration and depression. He'd almost given up on everything at one time, but thankfully he'd stumbled on the fact he could make things grow and help people with that talent. He always had to move on before those he lived near realised he wasn't aging and that his talent was fuelled by magic. But it made life bearable.

It was lonely though. He could never get close to anyone. It hurt too much when he moved on. But then he'd discovered Christmas, and it was something that helped him get through the rest of his year. The thought that, for this short period, he could be with people and share in the fun and the joy ... it was magical.

It's why he'd started up his Christmas tree farms all those centuries ago. It meant he could keep that feeling with him all year. Even in this country where the seasons were all turned around and it was summer when it should be winter.

It was beautiful though – although not right now, after the mess Mother Nature had dropped on him a few days ago.

He glared at the ruined field. Then up at the sky.

It was crystal blue, not a whisper of the storm that had caused the disaster in this newly sown field. Just the sun, beating down on him mercilessly as he worked.

But that was the weather here all over – unpredictable. Even after ten years of living on this farm in the Central Highlands of Tasmania, he hadn't got used to it.

He still wasn't sure why he'd come to a place where it rarely snowed and was hot at Christmas, but he had. The feeling inside him, the one that always told him it was time to move, made it impossible to go anywhere else. So he'd journeyed here and bought a derelict property and turned it into a successful Christmas tree farm; one of only three in Tassie.

He also grew other seasonal produce and had a good fruit orchard too.

Or *had* had a good fruit orchard. Many of those trees had been stripped of leaves, fruit and buds by the storm. It would take months to repair the damage. He'd planned to get started right after he fixed this field and planted the pine tree seedlings that were slated to be his crop of Christmas trees in four to five years.

Which was why he had to get this done soon. He didn't want to miss the summer growing season. If he did, he'd have nothing but four footers to sell in four years' time.

Which wasn't at all acceptable!

He was known for his six to eight footers. He couldn't give his customers less.

He ignored his stinging hands and the ache in his shoulders from hours of digging and carrying and dumping the stones and rocks and other debris scattered across his field and returned to work.

Not long after, a rumbling jangling sounded behind him and he turned to see Daphne driving up in his ute with the now empty trailer.

She waved at him and smiled. And even though he was hot and sweaty and not a little annoyed at having to be out here doing this when he should be tending to the trees they were going to sell this year, he smiled and waved back.

Daphne didn't deserve his grumpiness. She'd lived a hard life and he was happy to do anything he could to make it a little easier. After her shit of a husband had just up and left, taking their life savings with him, leaving her with two young boys and another on the way, she deserved every good thing he could do for her.

Given his situation, he knew he shouldn't have let any of them get so close to him, but after coming across her labouring so bravely alone in the old stockman's cottage with no power or hot water, her boys crying because they didn't know what to do, he had to help. Then it had just seemed natural to renovate the stockman's cottage to make it a lovely place for her and the boys, and to offer them jobs because they needed them. The closeness thing had just kind of happened without him realising.

Now he had Daphne and her boys in his life, he couldn't imagine having to do without them. Although, sometime in the next five to ten years, when they noticed he wasn't aging, he would have to tear himself away from this little accidental family.

It would tear a hole in his lonely heart.

He would grieve their loss, but he would move on. He

just had to hope he had as long as possible with them and didn't give himself away before then.

Thankfully, the magic that lived deep inside him and seeped out into the growing things around him, helping them to thrive, did so in a non-flamboyant way. A way that in this modern world where people didn't believe in magic anymore, he could pass off as a very green thumb. People didn't blink over the furfie he told over a secret fertiliser mix that helped his Christmas trees and other produce grow so quickly. They just kept trying to get him to sell his secret formula, and took any advice he gave when he refused to sell it to them.

The ute pulled up beside him and Daphne hopped out, her brown bob glinting in the sunlight. Instantly her hands went to her hips and she scowled at him. "Trip O'Dem! Did I not tell you stop and drink a bottle of water before I left with that last load? Just look at the state of you."

Oh crap. He'd forgotten about the water the moment she'd driven away. He'd just wanted to get back to fixing his field. He had to start the planting. Had to. He was running out of time.

"Did you even drink any of the water in that bottle I gave you?"

He grimaced a smile at her. "Umm, maybe." He'd meant to take a mouthful, but given how dry his mouth was, not to mention a little lightheaded, maybe he hadn't. When the need to work came on him, it kind of took over. It was difficult to explain that to other people, especially Daphne, who seemed to like to mother him as much as she mothered her boys.

She reminded him a little of someone, but he couldn't think who. Maybe his own mother.

He winced as pain spiked through his head at the

thought of a woman he couldn't remember. Thankfully Daphne didn't see it – she had bent to swipe something off the ground.

She straightened, and, with thunder in her eyes, shoved it in front of his face. "No, you didn't. It's full. See! You just dropped it on the ground the moment I left, didn't you? Without even opening the cap!" She shoved the bottle into his chest and let go – he had to drop the fork to grab it. "Well, why are you staring at me like that? Drink up. The whole thing. And I expect you didn't stop to eat the sand-wiches I packed for you either?"

He looked sheepishly at her as he unscrewed the cap on the bottle.

She sighed loudly then poked a finger at him. "How you managed to survive before I came into your life, I have no idea."

"Neither do I."

His words seemed to placate her, because her mouth twitched as if she was fighting not to smile. Hands back on her hips, she said, "Well. You need to eat. Now."

"I'd just like to finish—"

"I'm not going to let you load up the trailer until you do." She shook her head at him.

"You don't need to baby me," he said, then took a swig of the water. Gods, the cool wetness felt so good sliding down his throat. He swallowed convulsively.

"If you don't want to be treated like a baby, then perhaps you should act your age."

Easier said than done, given he'd never met anyone else who was well over a couple of thousand years old – at least, he guessed he was – and so had no benchmark to judge how someone his age was supposed to act. So he mostly just tried to act like a thirty-something human man, which was the age he resembled.

He finished drinking the water, wiped his hand across his mouth and held out the empty bottle. "Happy?"

She rolled her eyes and pointed at the Esky she'd placed by the fence that morning. "Sandwiches."

Knowing it was pointless to argue, he went to the Esky, pulled out the Tupperware container – it contained two big sandwiches filled with ham, cheese and salad, just the way he liked it – put the lid back on the Esky and then used the sturdy container as a seat.

He bit into the sandwich and couldn't help the groan of pleasure that rumbled in his throat.

She threw him an 'I told you so' smile along with an eyebrow twitch that said, 'but what did I expect, you male-idiot', and then went to work, picking up the smaller branches and rocks and putting them in the trailer.

By the time he'd finished the two sandwiches, she'd cleared half of what he'd freed from the mud and was trying to drag one of the bigger branches over to the trailer.

"Here, let me get that." He reached for the branch.

She dropped it. "Oh, Trip. Your hands!"

He looked down. They were red-raw and blistered. No wonder they stung. But he'd been so focused on work, he hadn't even taken the time to look at them. "They're fine," he said. And they would be. He healed quickly. But that wasn't really the problem right now. He couldn't let the blisters pop or his skin crack and bleed. It would be disastrous if it did.

He'd been careless. Stupid.

He stomped over to the ute and pulled his thick work gloves out of the glove box. He should have put them on this morning, but he'd been too focused on getting started and hadn't thought beyond that. Thank the Gods Daphne had noticed now. He hated to think of what might have happened if she hadn't.

His blood should never come into contact with soil. It was another thing he didn't know the why of, just the certainty of the unfortunate consequences that would follow if it did.

It was the reason he never forgot his gloves. Even his preoccupation with getting to work shouldn't have made him forget. It was too important. So why had he?

He didn't know.

He really wasn't himself today.

"Trip, what are you doing?" Daphne grabbed his arm as he pulled on the second glove. "You can't be thinking to do more work!"

Trip stared at her as if she was the one being unreasonable. "Of course I am. This field needs to be cleared and then ploughed and the soil prepared so I can plant the seedlings by the end of the week."

"You can't do all that in a few days! Especially with those hands. You need to come back and let me clean and put some salve on them. Then rest for a day or two. When Charlie gets back from Launceston with the replacement fake-snow making machine, he can take care of this."

"No. I need to do this now." He yanked his arm from her tenacious grip, ignoring the look of worried confusion on her face. "Just let me work." He stomped to where he'd dropped the fork.

"But ... what's the hurry? If you don't get it done until next week or the week after, it will still be fine. We'll still have trees in four to five years, especially given how good you are at growing them."

"No, it has to be done now." He grabbed the fork and

shoved it under a rock, groaning at the effort to lever the bloody thing out of the sucking mud.

"Trip! Stop."

"I can't."

"Why?"

"You don't understand."

"No, I don't. Why don't you tell me?"

He opened his mouth to explain, but all he could do was make a croaking sound. Because he couldn't explain. He just knew it had to get done. He was running out of time. "I just … I just need to get back to work."

"Trip!"

"Isn't it time to go pick up Gideon? Don't you need to take him to basketball practice?"

She glared at him. He glared at her.

Finally, she threw her hands up in the air. "I give up. Fine. Let those blisters pop. Get sepsis. See if I care." She stomped off across the field towards the far gate – it was the closest one to the stockman's cottage, which was nestled in the hill just beyond the neighbouring field of Christmas trees. As she got to the gate, she turned and shouted, "Just don't come running to me when you wake in the night with a fever and need help."

"I won't," he shouted back, knowing that, of course, in the event of that unlikely scenario, she would come running faster than a speeding bullet. Superman had nothing on her when it came to helping others.

The woman truly was a gem.

She opened the gate, then slammed it behind her, the clanging sound of metal against metal making birds fly up out of the nearby gumtrees in a flurry of squawking and flapping wings.

Daphne didn't even look up at them as she disappeared

amongst the Christmas pines that were for next year's buyers.

Trip grimaced. Crap. He'd really upset her. He'd have to do something nice later. He'd think over what while he worked.

Shoving his hands more firmly into the protective barrier of the gloves, he got back to it.

CHAPTER

THREE

Twenty minutes after hopping out of bed, the steaming hot shower having beaten the trembling from Ilia's muscles and the cold from her bones, she stood in front of the mirror, dressed, teeth cleaned, and stared at her mop of wet, waist-length dawn-gold hair, darkened into an almost normal light brown by the water. It would spring into a riot of unruly curls the minute it started to dry, so she tied it into a messy knot and headed downstairs.

Her pink bunny slippers slapped quietly on the carpet runner of the stairs. It always made her smile when she shoved her feet into them. She wondered if Tamuel had known it would when he gave them to her not long after they returned from Roma at Easter. Violetta had been appalled by the gift, telling him it was inappropriate given how and when Ilia had been brought back to life, but Ilia didn't think so. It was kind of funny how grotesquely cute they were – virulently pink with ears so floppy they flipped around wildly when she walked.

She bent, giving the ears a little pat as she made it to the bottom of the stairs, then straightened and stopped dead.

"What the Hells!"

It looked like the house had vomited up Christmas decorations. There was a massive pine tree opposite the front door, its limbs reaching up to the vaulted ceiling and decorated with bows and baubles and lights. If this wasn't enough to scream 'Christmas is coming!', wreaths had been hung and wound around every available surface, lights twinkling in their faux-pine depths. It was then she noticed a wreath with colourful baubles, bows and lights had been wound around the staircase banister. She'd been so busy staring at the bobbing bunny ears on her slippers that she somehow hadn't noticed.

"Hells."

Tamuel had said Jules was mad about Christmas, but she hadn't thought it would be like this. Jules had been too ill and tired with morning sickness last year to do more than slap up a few decorations and a small Christmas tree. Although, she had forced Bas, Tamuel and Korinna to watch multitudes of candy-cane sweet Christmas movies with her. Given Ilia had been trapped in the gem, which at the time had been fixed inside Tamuel's chest like it was in hers currently, she'd been privy to everything he saw. Unless she purposefully tuned out, she'd had no choice but to watch. Tamuel had said she should tune out if she didn't like it, but given she only had the energy to do that for short periods of time, periods she kept for when he and Korinna had sexy times together – which was a lot! – she hadn't had the energy to withdraw for so-sickly-it-made-her-want-to-vomit movies.

The only one she could stand had been Scrooged – that Bill Murray was kind of cute in a scruffy way and it was pretty funny when he was being slapped around by the tiny and violent Ghost of Christmas Present.

Not to mention, she could kind of see his point of view. Of course, that was before he'd turned into a sap at the end of the movie, got his second-chance love and learned his lesson, which he then proceeded to share via a lecture to the viewer, as if they hadn't been able to figure the moral out for themselves.

Socrates had a bloody lot to answer for when he introduced moralistic thought to the world.

"Bah humbug!" she muttered to the cheerily blinking lights surrounding her before stomping down the hallway.

It too had Christmas cheer in abundance, as did every room she passed. Was there no place she could escape to except for her bedroom to get away from all this? Maybe the kitchen—

"Hells," she muttered again as she stopped in the kitchen doorway.

It hadn't been spared from the Christmas 'cheer' as she'd hoped. All around her, wreaths and twinkling lights hung and there was a veritable elves-reindeer-Santa palooza on the dresser *and* the window-sills by the breakfast nook. "And I'm expected to eat in here?" she muttered.

"Good morning. Say morning to Aunty Ilia, Dawn."

She whipped around. Jules stood at the kitchen sink, baby Dawn in her arms, waving at her. Well, not so much of a baby anymore – she was almost eight months old.

Trying not to wince at the Christmas apron Jules wore, which bore a winking cartoon Rudolf with the words 'Naughty *and* Nice' under him, Ilia forced herself to enter.

"You're up early."

"Not really." She always woke at sunrise, even now the

days were getting longer and daylight came earlier and earlier.

"You're the first to see all the Christmas decorations," she said proudly. "What do you think?"

"Umm ... None of this was here last night before I went to bed."

"I know. I wanted it to be a surprise for everyone," Jules said, satisfaction filling her voice. "I got up during the night and used my magic."

Ilia gasped. "You didn't just ... poof this into existence, did you?" Because if she had, that meant Jules had more than Goddess-given powers. It meant she had the power to create worlds. And destroy them.

Jules chuckled. "My bank account wishes I could! No – I bought it all. Haven't you noticed all the packages arriving over the last few months?"

"Nope." She'd been too busy trying to find a way to separate herself from Dawn and to help Korinna and the others find Triptolemus. "I've spent most days down in the library."

Jules threw up her hands. "You see! This is exactly why I wanted to do this. We've all been so busy concentrating on finding the elusive Triptolemus, we've forgotten all about why we're doing it in the first place."

"I thought it was so he could tell us what big bad is coming for us and how to stop it. And to help undo the blood-curse on his and Korinna's magic."

"Well, that of course. But isn't it also to preserve this?" She waved her hand around.

"What? A home?"

"No ... well yes. And all it encompasses – family, friendship and love."

Which is exactly why she hated it – it reminded her of everything she'd lost and was never to have.

Jules didn't notice her bleak expression though, her attention on Dawn as she jiggled her up and down, making the baby giggle. "But I meant we also need to preserve fun. We need to celebrate the joyous things, otherwise, what's the point of living?"

Ilia really didn't have an answer to that – living for her had just been existing for so long, and still kind of felt like that, despite the new life she'd been given.

Jules tipped her head and shook it sadly. "You see! You need to be reminded about fun."

Ilia glanced around her. *This* was fun?

Jules waved her hand expansively. "Et voila! Great start, isn't it?"

Start? This was just a start?

"I have so many fun activities planned leading up to Christmas." Activities? She hid her shudder as Jules spun around and said, "What do you think?"

"It's ..." She swallowed hard. "Very bright. Cheery."

"Oh, I'm glad you think so. I wasn't certain the tree in the foyer was big enough or that I'd hung enough lights."

"No, there's enough. Of everything."

Jules beamed at her. "I love Christmas so much."

"Really?" she drawled. "You wouldn't be able to tell from this."

Jules laughed and said, "I know it's a lot ... but go big or go home, right?"

"Umm ... right. But ... I thought witches were supposed to celebrate Yule."

Jules made a pffing noise. "Given I didn't have any power for most of my life, I missed out on all the things the rest of the Coven enjoyed this time of the year – especially heading OS to where it's cold and snowing so they could properly do all the rites and rituals. So I took Christmas as my own." She reached for a bowl as Dawn jigged in her arms, the baby almost knocking the rice cereal onto the floor.

Ilia rushed forward and grabbed it before it landed. "I bet your Coven wasn't happy about that."

Jules took the cereal from her then pulled a face. "Thanks – and no, they weren't. They gave Violetta a really hard time for letting me get so invested in it, but she never let that stop me. She wanted me to have something that was mine, so she did all she could to celebrate with me."

"That was ... nice of her."

Jules nodded. "More than nice. It showed me how much she loved me, which was the best present I could have every year. And now I have my magic, I can go to town like I've always wanted. I can't wait for Dawn to see the choo-choo in the lounge room. And if you like the lights in here, wait until you see what I've done outside. I think it's pretty special."

"Must be," Ilia said, thinking she'd have to wear very dark sunglasses if she was to venture outside any time in the next month. "Umm, does the Christmas cheer extend all the way down to the library?" Hells, she hoped not.

"No." Jules grimaced. "I tried one year to put a Christmas tree down there but the ghosts kept stealing the decorations and hanging them off the chandeliers and turned the tree into Yule logs which they shoved into various corners, so I never tried again. Although, now I have my magic I might be able to set a spell that stops them. Do you think I should?"

"No!" Jules blinked at the almost-shouted word. Ilia smiled hastily, trying to cover. "I mean, you don't want to upset the ghosts or your Coven do you? The library is a witching space, so maybe it's best not to open that can of worms."

Jules sighed. "You're probably right." She glanced around and smiled. "Maybe I'll just put a few more decorations in here to brighten it up a little more."

A little more? If it got any brighter, she'd have to start wearing sunglasses in here too. But instead of showing her dismay, she turned to the coffee machine and said, "Now you have your powers, shouldn't you give this away and embrace Yule as the rest of your Coven do?" She glanced up to see Jules staring at her.

"Are you crazy? And miss all this?" She gestured at the house around her.

"Of course, what was I thinking?"

"How could I deprive Dawn? I want her to have the best of both worlds. Besides, it's just so joyful."

"Yes." The kind of joyful that shoved itself down your throat and choked you. But she couldn't say that to Jules or give away just how much she didn't like it – Jules had been so wonderful to her since Oestra, helping her in many ways to acclimatise to this new life and being so good about the fact Ilia was linked like she was to Dawn. She'd also been a great learning partner, given both of them now had magics they'd never had use of before.

All the Stevens had been amazing in fact. She'd sooner eat one of the Christmas wreaths than hurt any of them with how she truly felt about anything.

Just then Dawn leaned out of her mother's arms towards Ilia, making grabbing motions with her hands. Jules laughed. "Can you hold her while I finish getting her rice cereal mush ready? She's extra impatient for it this morning – mummy's breast milk just wouldn't do, would it,

Sweetums?" she said to the baby, rubbing noses with her, making Dawn chuckle. Then the baby leaned away and put her hands out towards Ilia once more. Jules laughed. "So impatient."

"As Her Majesty dictates," Ilia said smiling. She took the baby, holding her close, breathing in the delicious scent of her – powder and breastmilk and something greener, fresher and incredibly warm; a smell that she could only describe as of the dawn. Which made sense given the Goddess' star she was born under and the reason for the name she'd been given.

"Why so hungry this morning?" she asked as she jiggled the baby, walking away from Jules to where Dawn's high-chair sat by the table.

Dawn lifted her chubby hands and cupped Ilia's face, looking up at her out of her big, indigo eyes with the gold of dawn's light flickering in their depths. Then she shook her head, expression serious in a way that only a baby with her magical heritage could.

"So this impatience isn't about hunger?"

She glanced at her mother – busily pouring boiled water into her dried cereal. She made a little sound of longing.

"So you are hungry?"

A nod. Then those remarkable eyes met hers again and she shook her head quickly.

"Ah, but it's not *all* about hunger?"

Dawn tipped her head, little mouth screwed sideways as if considering the question, then tapped her head.

"You had a dream?"

A shake. Then she touched Ilia's brow and cocked her head in question.

"My dream?" An enthusiastic nod. "You want to know

about my dream? But I can't remember." Even as she said it, images flickered to life in her mind. Not of her sons as she'd thought the dream must be about, but the man who featured in her dreams more and more often.

In her mind she saw him now as clear as day, the man waking in a snow-frosted pine forest, confusion and pain on his handsome face; walking aimlessly, heavy bags slung over his shoulder as he tried to find shelter and answers; falling into a depression when no answers were forthcoming, his efforts to remember only bringing incredible pain that drove him to unconsciousness time and time again.

Time passed, dark and bleak, with him wandering, lost, alone, bereft – oh, how she knew those feelings! Time shifted again before the memory of them could grab too tight a hold, then the image stopped, to show him being given shelter by an impoverished farmer and his family; it showed the moment when he'd touched the few seeds the farmer had left to him, dried husks that would never have grown, but at his touch, sprang into seedlings and multiplied. And with their growth, a new passion inside him was born.

After helping the farmer and others sow the seedlings into one bumper crop after another, the man had to strike out on his own when the community realised he was not aging and that his talent with growing things had more to do with magic than a green thumb. Despite the help he'd given them, they'd come after him with pitchforks.

These scenes were repeated over and over in different places, a flickering cascade of images that made her slightly nauseated. Then it settled into an image of him wearing light khaki shorts, a dark blue t-shirt, feet encased in heavy work boots – modern clothing – as he worked under a hot sun, sweat glistening on his brow.

She swallowed hard. "Are you seeing this too?"

A firm nod.

She wanted to ask why the baby saw the man too when she never had before, but the questions that popped out were, "Who is he? And why do I keep seeing him?"

Dawn blinked at her, then flattened her hand against Ilia's brow.

The kitchen swirled around her, fading to nothing. She was flying high above the ground.

No, not flying. Falling.

The ground rushed up to meet her.

She screamed as she fell into the dream she'd woken from that morning.

FOUR

The scream rang out across the tops of the trees, echoing back to Trip from the hills that surrounded his property. The birds that had settled into trees across the way took flight again, squawking and flapping around in frightened disaray as they flew from the source of the trouble. Yet, there seemed to be no source as the scream rang all around from every direction.

He stood there for a while, looking for the source of the sound, but there was nothing. Probably just possums mating – they really did make a horrible sound. Although, it was strange they'd mate during the day, given they were nocturnal animals. The scream didn't repeat and the birds settled down into the trees on the other side of the field as if nothing had disturbed them.

Shrugging, Trip arched to stretch his back. Sweat stung his eyes – he wiped his arm across his forehead but the sweat was back a minute later.

He filled the trailer, made a run to the empty field

behind his house where they'd dumped the rest of the stuff – he'd keep the wood for a bonfire for winter and maybe build a fence from the rocks? – then returned with the empty trailer and kept going.

The sun seemed to get even hotter as he made two more runs with a full trailer before returning to finish the last of the clean-up. His shirt was wet with sweat, his hands were stinging inside the gloves and his socks were so wet he was certain his feet were turning into prunes inside his boots. At some stage though, he'd thankfully stopped sweating. Although, his mouth was incredibly dry. He should stop and have one of the bottles of water Daphne had left. He'd grab one after he cleared this section.

He dug the spade into the soil, but almost fell as the world swayed before him, the horizon shimmering in a way it shouldn't at this hour of the day. Shadows had grown long across the paddock and the heat of the sun had faded. He stood there, clinging to the spade, suddenly burning hot and yet shivering at the same time. And his tongue felt large and sticky, almost like it didn't belong in his mouth.

Crap! His thoughts were sluggish, but not so much that he didn't realise what he'd done to himself. He was seriously dehydrated. He needed water. There were more bottles in the Esky. Which he'd put in the ute after he'd eaten. He just had to make it there.

He made it a couple of steps, using the pitchfork to steady himself as the world wheeled around him. Almost there. Just had to round the trailer and get to the door.

He stumbled on the overturned earth he'd worked earlier, arms pinwheeling as he tried to re-balance himself. But he bounced into the wheelbarrow he'd left leaning against the edge of the trailer, tripped over his own feet and smacked his head.

The loud dull clang of head hitting the side of the ute rang through the twilight around him as he stumbled. No, no, he couldn't let the blood-soaked kerchief hit the soil.

Somehow, he managed to catch himself on the trailer before he fell to the ground.

He stood there, shaking, taking in deep, unsteady breaths. Head spinning from the knock, he steadied himself and stared at the horizon to try to settle his vision. He couldn't pass out here – there was no phone reception and Daphne wouldn't be back for hours to check on him.

He tried moving, but his head rang and something wet dripped across his eye and onto his cheek.

Shit, no!

He grabbed his kerchief from his pocket and pushed it against his forehead, willing the bleeding to stop.

But it didn't and the kerchief was soon soaked through. He shoved it in his pocket and hauled his t-shirt off – a more than exhausting exercise, indicating just how badly dehydrated he'd let himself become – and pushed it against his head. It wasn't good enough. Blood dripped onto his chest.

Hells. He couldn't let it touch the ground.

He had to move. Had to get in his ute.

Using the trailer as a guide, he edged his way forward slowly. The world flipped sideways. The pressure in his head increased. He kept going.

A breeze had blown up as twilight settled around him, cooling his heated, dry skin.

Almost there. Almost there. The door to the ute stood open just a metre ahead. He could get there. He could. He just had to let go of the trailer and take two steps.

He let go, lifted his leg and ...

The ground rose up to greet him. His gloved hands

splayed out before him, hitting the dirt first. Then his arms gave way and he landed face first in the dirt.

There was a hiss as his blood hit the soil and sank in.

Before he could push himself up, greenery sprung up all around him, racing across the field until it was full of swaying fruit trees, South Esk Pines and an abundance of all the plants he'd ever grown in his life – a veritable garden of Eden.

No-no-no-no-no! How was he going to explain this?

He began to push upright. Then froze.

A woman, in a flowing gown the colour of night just before dawn, walked towards him through the greenery. She was short and curvy, with curling long blonde hair that somehow held dawn in its depth. She stared around her, her plump mouth puckered in a little 'oh' of surprise as if she'd never seen anything like this before – in truth, she probably hadn't.

She drew near to him and he sucked in a breath – in eyes that were the darkest purple lit by sunlight, he could see pain like a never-ending scream.

How could she have endured so much pain?

A voice he knew from his dreams whispered, *"Drink. You must drink of her blood. For she is made of dawn's light and the rejuvenating qualities of birth and rebirth. She is of the eternal stuff of life now, like the Old Gods; like you were. Her blood holds magic and knowledge of ancient things within. Drink of her and you will be returned."*

What the fuck?

"Drink. Drink her now. She has come to you. She is the one we've waited for."

"No!" He would never do such a thing.

"No?" the woman questioned as she stopped next to an

apple tree that held a single apple. Her gaze raked over his form. "You can see me?"

He nodded.

"Holy crap!"

"Holy crap indeed." He couldn't keep talking to her from this position flat on his stomach in the dirt. Sucking in a breath, he pushed to his knees slowly. The world moved again but somehow she remained steady. Solid. He concentrated on her and managed to sit back on his haunches without falling over. "Who are you?"

She just stared at him then plucked the apple from the tree and took a bite, brows rising a little as she chewed. He watched her, mouth dry, as she continued to eat the fruit that had been born from his blood and whatever magic happened when it touched barren soil. The action was mesmerising, stoppering all thought until there was nothing but a core left.

"Who are you?" he asked again.

She dropped the core on the ground beside her and said, "The question is, who are you? And how did you do this?" Her gaze left him to take in the still-growing trees and plants around them.

"I didn't …"

Her gaze collided with his once more.

The breath left his lungs at the impact. Her eyes, they were extraordinary. He'd not seen eyes like that since—

He clutched his head as pain spiked through him.

"Are you okay?"

"I'm … fine," he managed after sucking in a shaky breath. He waved at his head. "Just hit my head, that's all."

Her gaze went to the cut on his brow. "Here, let me take care of that." She waved her hand. There was a small breeze of air around his brow and then the pain of the cut was gone.

"Thank you. Although I wished you were here earlier to stop this from happening," he said, giving up all pretence that he had nothing to do with the magical growth. She would notice pretty quickly that as the blood stopped flowing, so the greenery stopped growing.

Her eyes widened as they flickered between him and the greenery. "Your blood. It did this." It wasn't a question; rather, it was said on a breath of horror. "Blood magic. You did this with blood magic." She took a step back, as if suddenly afraid of him. "I can't be here. I can't be a part of this." She turned.

He held up his hand. "No. Stop. Don't go!"

But it was too late. She'd already disappeared.

"What the fuck?" The words exploded out of him as he scrambled to his feet, suddenly not the least bit dizzy. "Where did you go? Who are you? And why should I drink your blood?"

He cried the words into the darkening sky, but there was no answer.

He stood there, the new greenery the only movement as it rustled in the breeze that had sprung up.

He must have imagined her. Yes, she was a result of a knock on the head and the worry about how he would explain to his neighbours, to Daphne and her boys, about his suddenly lush and fertile paddock.

Even so, he couldn't stop himself from going to where she'd stood, to find the imprint of high heels in the grass and the apple core where she'd dropped it.

She *had* been real.

But what in all the Hells did it mean? And what was he supposed to do now?

Even more importantly – how was he supposed to explain this field to Daphne and the boys? Because he sure as shit knew there was no way of keeping it from them.

Perhaps they would believe in Christmas miracles?

CHAPTER

FIVE

Ilia reeled as the sensation of falling suddenly stopped. She couldn't believe she'd screamed like that. But it had been terrifying, so ... kind of justified. Her heart still pounded in her chest though, her breath sawing through her lips.

"Get your shit together, girl," she panted.

She breathed slow and deep until things started to settle around and inside her. As it did, she gathered her spiralling thoughts: whatever this was, it wasn't a dream.

There was no fogging around the edges, no flipping from one place to another, no sense of timelessness. Plus, the falling had felt real.

In fact, all of it was too real, too vivid. And as she breathed in deeply, she realised it wasn't only sound and image she was getting, but also scents.

A vision? Was this a vision?

Yet it didn't quite feel like that either.

Then what was it?

Did it matter?

No. She had to stop wasting brain energy on questions

she couldn't answer and concentrate on what she'd been brought here to witness.

The man from her dreams was in front of her, digging up a muddy field, his entire attention on what he was doing.

It was strange to see him in this way. So tired and frustrated and … driven. He was usually pretty jovial in the dreams she remembered, despite the loneliness that always seemed a part of him.

She hovered over the scene for a time, watching him work. He worked long and hard, never stopping even though he was sweating up a storm and must feel the effects of the hot day.

She dropped closer when he tripped, hitting his head on the ute.

He tried to get in but didn't make it. Ilia wished she could help him as he fell to the ground, the cut on his brow bleeding profusely.

Then suddenly, green things began to spring out of the ground – trees and bushes and flowers of all types, shapes and sizes – and within minutes, the muddy, ruined paddock had turned into a strange garden; a mix of orchard, vegetable garden and pine forest.

It was so lush and inviting, she wanted to go down and explore it; find out how it had suddenly come to be. The male seemed to be the source – but how?

Then suddenly, as if just thinking it made it real, she stood on the field, the springiness of lush grass under her feet, the scent of wildflowers and summer fruits hanging heavy in the air around her.

What the fuck?

Despite her confusion, she couldn't help walking closer to the man. He was looking wildly around, then he sucked in a breath.

"No!" He shouted, seeming to stare right at her.

"No?" She stopped next to an apple tree that a single apple had grown on, gaze raking over him as his raked over her. "You can see me?"

He nodded.

"Holy crap!"

"Holy crap indeed." His voice, deep with a slight huskiness, wove around her, reminding her of the warmth of a fire in the hearth and the enticing scent of cinnamon and honey. *Home. He is home,* her mind whispered. The whisper stole all other thought.

He didn't seem to be struck so dumb though. He pushed to his knees slowly, swayed a little, his remarkable eyes fogging before refocusing on her with a kind of desperate need that made her shiver. "Who are you?"

She didn't respond, didn't quite know how to. She looked down, noticed she had plucked the lone apple from the tree, and without thinking, took a bite. Oh by all that was holy! She'd never tasted anything so delicious. Sweet and tart and crunchy and juicy. It was perfect – and exactly what she needed. She ate greedily until there was nothing left but the core. Nothing had ever satisfied her quite so much as that apple.

And all the time she was hyper aware of him watching her with something in his eyes that made her heart expand in her chest with a deep warmth she'd never felt before.

"Who are you?" he asked again.

"He's not ready for you to tell him yet," the voice in her mind – a voice she'd heard in her dreams – said. It was right. *She* was barely ready for this – whatever it was. And yet she wanted to know him.

She dropped the core on the ground beside her. "The

question is, who are you? And how did you do this?" Her gaze left him to take in the still-growing trees and plants around them.

"I didn't ..."

Her gaze returned to him, and she noted that he was still bleeding, his face pale, eyes fogged with pain and exhaustion. Blood dripped from his chin, onto the ground. One drop.

Around her the trees and plants grew again, but slower than before.

He clutched at his head as if in severe pain.

"Are you okay?"

"I'm ... fine," he said on a shaky breath, obviously anything but fine. He waved at his head. "Just hit my head, that's all."

Her gaze went to the cut on his brow. "Here, let me take care of that." She waved her hand, using a spell she'd learned from Bas. A small breeze blew up around them, weaving around his head as magic sparked over his cut. As it went to work, she couldn't help but truly look at him – for he was so much more real now than he'd ever been in any of her dreams.

He was a big man, even kneeling in the dirt. Her mouth dried as she took in the breadth of his shoulders, the bulge of his pecs and biceps under his t-shirt, the way his sweat-damp hair clung to his forehead and how his excessively long dark lashes framed his leaf-green eyes. Most males, Gods and human alike, could suck it as far as she was concerned – except for Tamuel and Bastien of course – but there was something about this man. And it wasn't simply that he was glorious. There was something else. Something that called to a place inside of her she'd thought long dead, and made it surge to the fore.

She longed to go to him, touch him, enfold herself in his arms and never let go. It was a wild thought, one she'd never had in her long life, not even when she'd thought herself in love with Mars. This was deeper and fuller and wider. It was like ... oh!

She sucked in a breath. It was a bit like the feelings she'd had for that brief moment of joy after giving birth, when she'd held her boys and knew she'd never love anything like she loved them.

What the ever-loving fuck?!

Something changed in his eyes and he straightened as the pain left him, her magic having done its work.

"Thank you." His lips tilted a little as he gestured at the new growth around them. "Although I wished you were here earlier to stop this from happening."

She gasped. Did he just infer what she thought he had? Her gaze flickered between him and the greenery. Down to the place his blood had hit soil. Green threads, like pulsing veins, sprang out from where the spot the drop of his blood had landed, branching out to become one with every plant and bush and scrub that had grown.

All her warm, fuzzy feelings fled before panic. Her mouth dried and breath froze in her lungs as she realised what had just happened – was still happening – right before her eyes.

"Your blood. It did this. Blood magic. You did this with blood magic." She took a step back, trembling. "I can't be here. I can't be a part of this." She swung around, wondering how the Hells she could get out of this vision-thing she was in.

At the thought, the lush field and the handsome man wavered and disappeared and she was back in the kitchen, little Dawn in her arms, the fresh taste of apple lingering on her lips.

What the Hells! Why had she seen that? Why had she been there to witness the use of blood magic?

He hadn't seemed evil. But if he used blood magic, he was.

And if that was true, why had Dawn shown him to her? Breathing hard as if she'd been running, she stared at Dawn. The baby didn't seem disturbed at all. "Did you see that?"

Dawn shook her head and tapped Ilia on the brow once more.

"Just me?"

Dawn nodded.

Well, that was a relief. "Why did you show that to me?"

Dawn covered her eyes and then uncovered them. "I needed to see it?" Dawn nodded. "But why did it seem so real?" The tartness of the apple was still so clear on her lips.

Dawn flattened her palm on Ilia's chest, then drew it away, fluttering her hands to indicate flying. "I astral travelled?" Well that made a bit more sense for why it had seemed so real. She'd actually been there.

Dawn made a cooing sound that caught Ilia's attention again.

Ilia leaned in and whispered, "I wish you could speak so you could tell me why I needed to see him like that. Why is he so significant?" Was he part of the big evil they were supposed to fight? It made sense given he'd used blood magic. She shuddered again.

Dawn's little forehead puckered and she stroked Ilia's cheek as if to soothe her.

Hells. She was pathetic. Shoving her fear aside, she

kissed Dawn's downy head and said, "It's not your job to soothe me, little one. I should be soothing you."

Dawn shook her head and patted Ilia's cheek.

The stubborn gesture made Ilia chuckle.

"It's remarkable how you communicate so well with her," Jules said, joining them with the bowl of cereal in her hands. "I wish I could understand her half as well as you do."

"It's the link," Ilia said, gesturing to the now-invisible magic thread that tied their life-forces together. It was part of the magic that had given her life, and had tied them together in the most inexplicable way ever since.

As well as sharing certain thoughts and emotions, she could understand the baby, and the baby could understand her, in a way that should be impossible. That was the up side. The down side was that the thread meant she could never go too far from where Dawn was. They'd found out the hard way how dangerous it was if one of them got too far from the other a month after Dawn's birth and Ilia's rebirth.

She rubbed her chest in memory of the sensation of her heart slowing and almost stopping the day Jules had taken Dawn to the Coven's paediatrician for a check-up.

Dawn's heart had almost stopped too before Tamuel and Korinna's quick thinking had saved the day.

Since then, they'd barely been more than the distance between the top floor of Stevens' House and the area where the Coven library lay underneath it.

Dawn reached for her cereal, almost knocking it from her mother's hand.

"So impatient," Ilia chided. She set the baby down in her highchair then returned to the coffee machine to continue making her espresso, leaving Jules to feed Dawn –

an exhausting process of avoiding grabby hands, singing 'here comes the choo-choo' and cleaning up the half of it that always seemed to dribble down the baby's chin. Despite how advanced she was in other areas, Dawn certainly hadn't mastered eating.

But Jules handled it the way she handled everything else – without fuss or nonsense and as if she'd been doing it all her life.

It was hard to watch, reminding Ilia she'd never got to do any of that with her sons.

She clenched the edge of the kitchen bench and tried to ignore the feeding behind her, fixing her attention on the coffee machine.

Come on, come on.

It seemed to be slower than usual. She just wanted her espresso – a truly magical invention the humans had created that was better than the nectar of the Gods – and then she could escape and think more clearly over what had just happened.

Something that was difficult to do in a room overstuffed with an excess of tinsel and glitter and winking lights that were starting to make her head pound.

Finally her espresso was done. She picked it up and breathed in the nutty-bitter aroma – glorious. The scent lit up her nerve-ends and chased away the last prickling cold that witnessing the use of blood magic had left behind. She sipped cautiously – even better than it smelled. This Columbian roast was better than the Costa Rican one Bas had sourced a few weeks ago.

Even so, the taste of apple lingered.

Hells. She'd eaten an apple made of blood magic! What might that have done to her? She closed her eyes and checked her magic and the flow of her aura, but didn't notice any changes. The only lingering effect was that she could still taste the apple clearly. She breathed out a long sigh.

"You okay?"

"Uh-huh," she said and bolted down the rest of her coffee, needing it to scald the taste of that delicious apple from her traitorous tongue. It didn't quite work, so she set up another cup. Hopefully two would do it. As it poured, she turned back to Jules and said, "I think I might go down to the library."

"This early? Is that wise? Especially alone. You know what happened last time."

As if she'd forget. The family ghosts, the ones that lived in the Melbourne Coven Library, which lay below Stevens' House, had been attracted to her right from the moment she'd ventured into the cavernous space a month after they'd returned from Roma. Thankfully she'd been with Tamuel and Korinna and they'd managed to chase the ghosts away before they did more than rush around her too fast. They'd thought it was just curiosity at first, but it became obvious pretty quickly it was something more than that, given they had to chase the ghosts away every time she entered the library.

Then she'd made the mistake of going down there by herself. She'd actually thought Bas was down there – but he'd slipped out via portal when Jules had sent him a text asking him to get more nappies, and so the place had been empty.

Except for her and the ghosts.

They'd rushed her as soon as she'd stepped off the bottom stair, taking her by surprise. One got through before she managed to throw up a shield, taking over her body. It had left her weakened for days after she'd eventually pushed it out – unfortunately not before it had made her eat and drink way too much. She didn't think she'd be able to look at chocolate or Fanta ever again.

She hid her shudder at the memory and said, "I'll be fine. You don't have to worry about me. I'm a big girl. Besides, I've been working on my shields since then with Bas and Tam. They're pretty strong now."

"Are you sure? I can come down now. Dawn is finished her breakfast – and I wanted to do some research on earth magics. I thought maybe if we could pinpoint the type of magic Triptolemus used, it might help us track him down. From what you overheard Demeter say, he was left with some of his magic."

"That's a good idea."

Jules beamed. "I thought so. It will be good to get a start on it before anyone else comes down to work."

"You want to bring Dawn down to the library?"

The few times the baby had been down there, she'd screamed loud enough to make the chandeliers shake.

"Umm, I could go wake Bas."

"Don't be silly. I know he, Tamuel and Korinna didn't get back until the middle of the night."

They'd been tracking down leads on Korinna's father. All they had to go by was a muddle of contradictory mythology and history about Triptolemus that didn't give them any clarity on exactly who or what he was. But the others weren't giving up despite the fact that the only clues they'd found were in texts that were supposed to be lost to the ages but somehow had found their way into the Stephens' library – Bas had a theory that Demeter was trying to give them some help in her very own special way. Of course, just simply helping them outright was some-thing she seemingly couldn't do!

It was infuriating. Even more infuriating because despite all the clues, and all the chasing down leads, all they'd learned so far was that Triptolemus wasn't a minor God in service to Demeter as so many believed.

Interesting perhaps, but hardly Realm-shattering. If Demeter really wanted to help them, why not give them something more definite about where he actually was. Unless, of course, even she didn't know.

She bit her lip. Maybe that was it. Maybe he was hidden so well, even the Goddess he served couldn't see him.

Then how the Hells were they going to find him?

She sighed heavily. Then rallied. She couldn't give up. Tamuel and Korinna hadn't given up on her and she wouldn't give up on them in their time of need. Korinna needed to find her father for answers. They all needed to find her father for answers. And for help figuring out what it was they faced in the future and how to defeat it.

At least they had the Eleusinian Mysteries Grimoire, which apparently Triptolemus had written. Despite that fact making his standing in the pantheons even more unclear, it had at least opened up a treasure trove of spells and diary-like entries thanks to Korinna's magically cursed blood. What it couldn't tell them was where he was now.

She wished she could be more help in tracking Triptolemus down, but apart from what she'd overheard Demeter and Persephone say on the matter, she'd been pretty much useless in the hunt for the ancient God/demi-God or whatever he was.

All she could do was keep going through the ancient texts they had in the library and see if there was something there they'd not found before. An almost-hopeless task given she had no true idea what the Hells it was she was looking for, either about Triptolemus and his whereabouts or what the big bad was that had forced Demeter to take all his memories and send him out into the world without ...

"Holy crap!" She slapped herself in the head. The man in her vision-dreams! He'd grown things with his blood. It was like what Korinna had done with the ring and her blood earlier this year. Maybe he hadn't used blood magic at all, like with Korinna, because he was the same as her.

Which meant ...

"That's what you were trying to show me!" she said to Dawn. "I was just too stupid to see it!" And so full of fear she'd stupidly thought a man with such gentleness in his eyes could be part of the evil they were meant to battle.

Jules stared at her. "Too stupid to see what?"

She shook her head. "I don't want to say anything in case I'm wrong. But I really do need to go down to the library. Now."

"But the ghosts—"

"Don't worry." She raised her shield with a wave of one hand. "See. I'm already protected." She didn't wait for Jules to respond, just chugged down her second espresso – even though she was now less worried about the taste of apple in her mouth – then ran for the stairs to the library.

If she was right, this would change everything. For Korinna. For her family. Even, maybe for her.

Because, if she was right and the dream-vision male was Triptolemus, then their search was over and they would soon have all the answers they'd been looking for.

And maybe then, she could fully concentrate on how to cut the life-force bond with Dawn and free them both.

CHAPTER
SIX

Ilia raced down the stone stairway, the slap of her bunny slippers echoing loudly through the stairwell.

Lights flickered on in the library as she entered, as they'd been spelled to do, so that by the time she took the last, cautious step into the space, it was fully lit by the bone chandeliers that hung from the arched stone and wood ceiling.

The ghosts rushed her as she came to a halt, their hands outstretched, pale eyes gleaming brightly in even paler faces.

She flinched as they bounced off the shield, their impact like something poking at her mind – not bad, but not exactly pleasant. They quickly regrouped and rushed her again. She put her hand out even though the shield would keep them at bay.

They bounced off it again. It didn't hurt, but it also didn't tickle – a little worse than the first time.

Obviously it affected her more than it affected them – they rallied and came at her again.

The shield held, but this time the impact was more

than a poke at her mind; it was a slap. She stumbled back a step, shocked at how much it hurt. She hadn't read anything about it hurting when things impacted a shield like that. Was this what it had been like for Korinna last year when they were in the Void with the Pompeii spirits battering at the shield she'd put up while she fought with Clodia?

Why hadn't she ever asked about that? Korinna's shield had begun to crack, but that had been under the double onslaught of huge magic. and the spirits trying to get to her. This wasn't that. So what was wrong with her shield?

Maybe she hadn't constructed it properly. And if that was true ... Hells, that meant they would probably get through.

She was so stupid to have tested it with nobody around. Should have waited for Jules. Even if she had to put up with the Christmas cheer that had been vomited all over the house.

One of the ghosts picked itself up from where it had been thrown faster than the others and came at her again. Hells. What was that spell Korinna had used to chase them away?

She couldn't remember, so giving in to impulse, she raised her hands and called on the power she was still only learning to use; power that still didn't feel like it belonged to her.

Pink and golden light sparked on the tips of her fingers, then flared brightly. And as it did, the glow in her chest started up again too. Bugger. But she didn't have time to worry about it now. She waved her hands, the power sparking again. "Come closer and you'll get a taste of this. And I promise, you won't like it." She was guessing of course. She had no idea if the light and power of the dawn would bother them at all, but given they lived mostly in the shadows, it was her best bet.

All of them stopped except the one that had come at her first. She willed the spell to spark out towards it, and as it flew across the space between her and the ghost, an arc of power from her chest flew along with it. The moment it touched the spirit, it began to writhe, its mouth open, screaming. Then it began to flicker, like bad reception on a TV. The other ghosts shrieked in terror and ran away, followed quickly by the one she'd hit, his form still flickering.

"Good. Run!" she yelled after them "There's more where that came from."

Actually, she wasn't sure there was. The magic – both in her fingers and chest – had disappeared as fast as it had come and left her trembling.

Hells. She wasn't used to using magic like this despite the training Violetta and Bas had been giving her and Jules. Whatever the glow was that emanated from her chest, it packed a powerful punch. Aside from her trembling limbs, she also felt weak and dizzy.

It must have something to do with the way she got her power. Maybe the baby was giving more than one aspect of her power. But, was she sharing it willingly or was Ilia stealing it without knowing?

Fuck!

She really needed another thing to worry about and try to figure out like she needed a chastity belt!

The bloody Gods were sadists, fucking with her once again. They asked for and took too much over and over and over in their need to play their stupid games and screw with those they thought of as 'lower beings'.

Someone needed to make them pay – she only hoped

one day that that someone would be her. Or, if not her, that she would be there to see it when they got what they deserved.

Her anger was a warmth growing in her chest. A warmth that heated to a blaze, brightening the space around her as it snapped and crackled, pushing to get out. "Crap. Not again. What the Hells is going on?"

Calming herself with breathing exercises had worked this morning, so she endeavoured to do that again, closing her eyes, breathing deeply and thinking calming thoughts.

An image of the man from her dreams, the one she thought might be Triptolemus, sprang into her mind, and as it did, the angry heat in her chest changed, its blazing edges softening to a welcoming warmth that filled her with calm and clarity.

And longing.

The sensation was so strong, air punched out of her and her eyes snapped open.

Just then, something began to rustle and whisper from the depths of the library. Something else made a horrible moaning sound, coming from the direction of the Black Magic and Dangerous Books section. Then a voice whispered from somewhere close by, *"Blood. Your blood. He drinks your blood."*

Hairs lifted on her arms and the back of her neck. "What?" She spun around, looking along the closest stack as far as she could see. "Who said that?"

There was no answer. She must have imagined it.

Shaking off the jitters, she started towards the area where the computers and reference shelves were.

"Blood. More blood. Blood for the drinking. Blood for the thinking. Blood that is life. Blood that is strife. Blood that is

giving. Blood that is taking. Blood that is destiny always in the making."

She stopped, fear whispering across her skin, drying her mouth. She wanted to run. But she couldn't. Wouldn't. She was sick of other beings playing with her for their own sick reasons. She had no idea how or why it was in some God's interest to torment her with her fear of blood magic, but she wasn't going to play their games. Squaring her shoulders she shouted, "Shut up! Just shut the Hells up. I don't want to hear anything more about blood or what it can do. If you don't have something to tell me that will help me find Triptolemus or free myself from Dawn, then just fuck right off and leave me alone!"

"Blood is your destiny." It was little more than an echo in the distance.

"No. It bloody well is not!" No pun intended of course. She snorted and then yelled, "Screw you!" The words rang around her, echoing through the library.

All other sound ceased. Even the moaning from the Black Magic and Dangerous Books section. Surprised that whatever it was had actually listened to her, she slowly turned and continued over to the reference shelves, centring her mind back on the job ahead.

All she had to do was find the right way to work the magical reference book Jules had been building ever since getting her powers back. If she could do that, and if the realisation she'd had upstairs was right, she'd have good news for Korinna and everyone by the end of the day.

She was glad to see that Jules had left the catalogue reference book on the desk in front of the shelves – she'd obviously added more to it yesterday; it seemed even thicker than before. She still had a lot of work to do to include links and references to every book, grimoire and magical object in the library, but she was well on her way. And it was easier to use than the online system, or poring through drawers and drawers of card catalogues.

But it could still be a bit tricky as she'd learned the hard way. If she didn't pose her question just right, or make certain her thoughts were concentrated on the one thing, then it sent her to grimoires and journals that were completely unhelpful.

The difference today was that she had what she thought was a current image of Triptolemus in her head. All she had to do was open the book, place her hands on the pages, and bring that image to mind with the right question that would lead her to him.

It shouldn't be difficult to think about him. She seemed to think of him more and more these last few weeks and now, after having astral travelled to him with Dawn's help, it took nothing at all to picture his handsome face. Or hear the sound of his voice. Or see the leaf-green of his long-lashed eyes.

Whoa, was it getting hot in here?

She wiped her hand across her brow and then reached for the reference book. Her hand trembled, fumbling on the latch.

She shifted her shoulders, trying to rid herself of the itch that chased between her shoulder blades and ran down her back, prickling and tightening between her legs. She squeezed her legs together and clenched her fingers hard against her palms until the biting sting of her fingernails digging into flesh helped to push away the unwanted sensations sliding through her.

Ridiculous to have that reaction for a man she'd never even met in the flesh. She'd long ago vowed never to give into that kind of need again; the consequences of the one and only time she had were just too high.

Never again.

So, stop being stupid and just open the damned book.

The sting of where her fingernails had bitten into her palm helped to keep the frisson of want at bay as she flipped open the reference book and put her hands on the pages. She filled her mind with his image – the one she'd seen only a short time ago – and posed a question as she had every day since coming here. Although, rather than the question being, "Where is Triptolemus?" this time it was, "The man in my vision, is it Triptolemus?"

The page under her hands warmed.

It had never done that before.

She snatched her hand back as a crawling sensation brushed across her palm and fingers.

Oh! The page was filling with writing – the names of treatises and pieces of information and the grimoire or book she'd find them in.

And every single one of them held the same name within the descriptive line:

Triptolemus.

Then her eyes caught on a particular section she'd never seen before.

Triptolemus: Golden God of the Harvest. He who made the Garden Gems from his tears mixed with a piece of Demeter's heart. Servant and partner of Demeter and Persephone here on Earth. Instigator of the Eleusinian Mysteries. Holder of the sacred blood.

The sacred blood? So she'd been right. It had been a property of the blood that enabled him to grow things, not blood magic.

Her knees dipped as relief rushed through her.

She forced herself to read on but then stopped as her gaze hit the words a few lines down:

Triptolemus – he and his line forever destined to be God Killers.

What? There was a prophecy about them being God Killers? But hadn't Tiberinus said she was tied to a prophecy about God Killers? She'd always assumed that was why her sons had been taken from her; and why Tiberinus had chosen her rather than another witch with far more power than she had, to power the HBG?

There couldn't be two prophecies about God Killers, could there? Or was it the same prophecy?

How entwined were they? She thought she was involved in this because Korinna and Tamuel were the only ones who could have freed her from the gem. But what if it was so much more than that? What if …

Her mouth dried.

No. Those feelings for the man in her dreams she'd been drowning in, the reason she kept dreaming about him – it was nothing but lust and the need to find him. Nothing more. Nothing deeper. Because she couldn't do deeper. Not now. Not ever.

How could she ever be a part of this amazing group of people and their close-knit family? No matter how much she might long for it, she couldn't have it. She was too broken. Too unworthy. The need for revenge that drove her too much a part of her. She didn't want to let it go; not for them, not for anything. It gave her purpose. But she wasn't so gone not to understand that if she stayed with them, that darkness inside her would mar their love, their friendship, their family.

She couldn't do that to them. She couldn't destroy something so good.

Which was just another reason why she had to separate herself from Dawn. Why she had to leave them, no matter what they said.

But if they found out about this connection, they'd be unlikely ever to let her go. They'd keep trying to bring her back to them because that's who they were. So she couldn't show this to them. She didn't want them to start to believe things that just couldn't be. It was already going to be difficult enough to leave given they already treated her like family. It would be so much worse if they thought her connected to them, to Triptolemus, in some deeper way.

But how could she hide this?

She slammed the book shut, losing the page with the words that caused the hairs on her nape and arms to stand up.

Closing her eyes, she intoned a spell:

> *"Hide this entry where no one can see.*
> *Hide it away, show no one but me.*
> *Three time three times three times three,*
> *By the power of dawn light, so mote it be."*

The power spiralled up, ruffling her hair, then fell to wind around the book. Something tightened, there was a pop and the spell fizzed away.

It was done.

She blew out a slow breath. She wished she could empty the knowledge from her own brain. But she couldn't. Damn the Gods and Goddesses and their machinations, tying her into them once again.

Eyes prickling with tears that had more to do with anger than anything else, she took in a shuddering breath, looked up at the ceiling and shouted, "Fuck you, whoever is responsible for messing with me like this. Fuck you and all your children. I don't know how, but somehow I will make you regret using me like this. I swear it."

Three rolling knocks sounded in the distance.

She stilled.

Shit.

Fuck.

But she hadn't used the word 'vow'. So why had the Eternal Well treated her rash statement like a sacred vow?

Bloody fucking Hells. Why did the universe seem to have it in for her?

Hot tears poured down her face, heated rage bubbled in her chest, the glow of her power shining through her skin once more. She wished she could just let it go, let it lash out at those who'd caused this pain, but she didn't know exactly who was involved beside Tiberinus – and she knew there were others involved. So no taking her revenge yet.

Besides, she had things to do first.

It took her longer this time to push the power back, to stop the glow in her chest, but once done, she whispered harshly, "Fine. I said I'd find him and I will. But then I'm done."

She opened the book again and put her hands on it, filling her mind's-eye with Triptolemus' image once more. "Just show me where he is."

CHAPTER
SEVEN

The woman smiled at Trip, her eyes, like the darkest purple-blue of the night sky, glinted at him with something secret and knowing. Her smile widened as she opened her mouth and licked the apple juice from her lips – the action gripped him in the groin and tightened his balls.

He groaned at the memory, hand tightening around his erect cock – a cock that seemed to spend more of its time erect than not, ever since he'd seen the woman in his field a few days ago.

Day or night, she was there, with him, the long gown that looked like something from Roman times draped over her, hugging in all the right places and showing off the shadow between her pert breasts.

In these daydreams – the ones that kept coming to him whether he wanted them or not – this was the moment she dropped the apple core to the ground and reached for the clips on her shoulders holding her gown together.

She didn't disappoint now.

With that knowing look, she slowly – so slowly and

sensually it stole his breath – undid those butterfly-like clips and let the gown fall, showing off skin the colour of rich cream and nipples swollen and softly pink.

Still smiling, she reached out her hand and said, "Triptolemus. I am here for you. Come. Drink of me and all will be well."

Even the pained dissonance that strange name – so like his, but not – caused every time she said it did nothing to rid him of the desire that heated his blood and made him want to touch, to take. And to want things he'd always stopped himself from wanting.

Connection. Belonging. Love.

Impossible things, but within these dreams, the impossible seemed to be within his grasp.

He rose to his feet, reaching for her and—

There was a loud bang and then a voice said excitedly, "Oh my God. Trip! Have you seen the field? Oh, God ... My eyes! My eyes!"

Trip snapped out of his daydream with a horrible jolt to see Daphne standing before him. She'd turned around and had her hands clasped to her head. There was a sound coming from her that sounded suspiciously like smothered laughter.

He quickly tried to tuck himself back into his pants – a difficult task given how swollen his cock was. Although, with her sudden entry – not to mention the laughter – it was quickly deflating. "Umm, well, it wasn't ... I mean ... I wasn't ..." His eyes lit on the box with the inflatable Santa and his reindeers that he was supposed to be working on for the Winter Wonderland in time for their first customers this weekend. He had been reading the instructions when the daydream had taken over and ... He coughed. "I was about to erect the inflatable."

"I think you were doing a good job of it too," she said on a definite snort. "Is your inflatable tucked away yet? It's rather awkward to talk to you like this." She turned before he could answer, her eyes alight with laughter.

"I didn't mean for you to see—"

"Well, obviously you didn't. Nothing to be embarrassed about though, as I tell the boys. Masturbation is a healthy part of life. I'm kind of glad to see you do it too."

"What? Really?" He blinked completely taken aback before his mind zeroed in on the last part of her statement. "What do you mean 'do it too'?"

She snort laughed. "Well, I think that would be obvious."

Oh, Gods! He didn't want to hear that. Daphne was like a sister. The last thing he wanted to think about was her doing *that*! Face as red as his Santa suit, he stammered, "I ... Umm ... Wh-what did you come racing in here for? Is something wrong?"

Her eyes lit up with excitement. "Oh. Yes. That's why I barged in rather than knocking." She began to pace, excitement in every step. He'd never seen her this way before. "It's just so wonderful. I can't believe it really, even though I saw it with my own eyes."

She looked at him expectantly. A sinking feeling gripped his stomach and tightened his chest. Oh no! Even so, he couldn't help but ask, "Saw what?"

"The boys saw it this morning and came to get me. It's a ... It's a ..."

"Christmas miracle?" Trip groaned inside as the words fell from his lips. They sounded lamer than he'd imagined. There was no way she would believe—

"Yes! It's a Christmas miracle. A true Christmas miracle!"

"Really?" he asked before he could stop himself.

"Well, you've obviously seen it if you're calling it that – and don't think that we won't have a conversation later about why you didn't tell us when you first saw it. But for now, I'm too excited to be mad at you. All that growth in that destroyed field. Trees and plants I've never seen before. And endangered South Esk Pines too! Plus there's fruit trees and other produce springing up everywhere. All grown in only a few days. It's our own Christmas miracle! Who would have imagined?"

"Umm ..."

"Isn't it exciting?" she asked, hands on hips, hair uncharacteristically dishevelled, brown eyes glowing with excitement and ... jubilation?

Exciting wasn't the word he had in mind. Terrifying was more to the point. "I just ... didn't think you believed in such things."

"As miracles?" Her eyes widened in surprise. "Of course I do. I know you, after all."

Shivers prickled down his spin and he stilled, his breath once again caught in his chest. Oh Hells. What did she know? "I ... Wh-what do you mean by that?"

She walked over to him and cupped his cheeks – her hands warm against the sudden chill in his skin. "You came into our lives like a miracle. Everything was lost and I didn't know how I was going to keep feeding the boys, let alone clothe them and get them to school. There wasn't enough work around here and I had no money to pick up and move elsewhere. I'd been sitting there crying after the boys were asleep, when my contractions started and I had no idea what to do or where to go and then ... you appeared. I was so afraid you were going to kick me and the boys out regardless of the fact I was about to drop a baby, but you didn't. You took control and got me to the hospital and looked after the boys and then, the biggest miracle, you offered us all jobs and a place to stay, then took us in while you fixed the stockman's cottage up so it was not only liveable but lovely. What do you call that if not a miracle?"

"Umm, being neighbourly?"

She choked on a laugh as she blinked tears from her eyes. "I had neighbours, and not one of them did anything for us when we were tossed out after my husband left and took all our money. You were the only one who helped, and you did so without even knowing us at all." Her hand dropped to his chest as she smiled up at him and said softly, "You made me believe in miracles that day and every day since."

"Well ..." What did a person say to that? He took her hand and held it in his. "You were a miracle for me too. I never knew how badly I needed a frie— an assistant like you. You take care of all the things I didn't like doing – housework, bookkeeping, managing the shop and helping with the cooking and baking of the goods we sell. And Charlie, well, he's taken to farming like one born to it. And without Harry and how savvy he is with computers and social media and the like, the business would not be what it is today. And Gideon, well ... I never knew how much joy a baby would bring."

Daphne chuckled. "Don't let him catch you calling him a baby. He's a big ten-year-old now."

"He sure is. And a born salesman to boot. I think we sold more in the shop last Christmas than we've ever sold before, and that's mainly up to him working there alongside you for the first time."

She smiled, wide and proud. "It was pretty special. But it would never have happened if you hadn't taken us in and treated us like family." She touched his cheek. "And we are, family."

He swallowed hard. "Yes." They were. And he couldn't ask for a better one. Even though in a few years, he'd have to say goodbye to them forever. But he didn't want to think about that now.

She cleared her throat and patted his hand. "Now, what are we going to do about this Christmas miracle?"

Hells. He'd hoped she'd got so side-tracked by their trip along memory lane that she'd forgotten. No such luck. "Umm ... What is there to do about it?"

She gestured expansively. "Get the word out, that's what! We can't keep this miracle to ourselves."

"Can't we?"

She gave him that look that made him feel like he was living on an entirely different planet to her. Although, maybe he had been – it would explain a lot.

"Of course not! Miracles like this need to be shared with the world."

"But do they?"

More of that look. "Are you serious?"

Like a cyclone bearing down on land was serious. He nodded slowly. "I just ... don't see how it will be of benefit to us."

"Of benefit to us?"

"Yes," he said slowly, landing on the 's' with an uptick that turned it into a question. "I mean, if we let people know, won't it bring reporters and tourists and ... attention." Attention he'd spent his life running away from.

"Well, that's the point."

"It is?"

"Yes. To spread the goodness of the miracle." She

nudged his arm. "You of all people should understand. You're Mr Christmas."

"I am?"

"Yes. You love spreading the Christmas cheer and good will. I mean, look what you do for our ticket holders every year when they come to cut their trees. They get an experience here that they don't get at other farms, with the tractor ride and costumes and the food and drinks you serve and the goodies we sell, not to mention the Christmas Wonderland decorations you set up from the carpark to the shop and inside the shop and the fake snow you spray around. It's a proper outing and puts people in the true spirit of Christmas."

"Yes, well, I like doing that."

"And letting people know about this Christmas miracle is just an extension of what you already do."

Except, it had giant, sticky strings attached. Namely, all the questions about how it happened and the scientists and government folk who would come down with legal documents and insist on doing tests. He just knew they would somehow end up tying it to him, and that would lead to him being carted away by army people or the Men in Black and locked away in a dark room to be experimented on.

Okay, maybe he'd watched too many sci-fi shows with Charlie, Harry and Gideon, but there *would* be consequences. Not little consequences but CONSEQUENCES. Not least of which would be he'd lose this little idyll and the family that was his even faster than he planned.

Daphne was looking at him, excited expectancy written large on her face.

"Is it really? I mean, there'll be reporters and people traipsing everywhere."

She waved that issue away. "The reporters will come,

take their footage, ask some questions and then go. We can deal with them."

"Can we?"

"Of course. And of course, they'll get the word out." Her eyes glowed as she began to pace in front of him again. "Just imagine. People will come flocking to see, to share in the miracle. They'll buy everything we have and we'll be booked out for the next ten years or more! Not to mention the tourists it will bring to the rest of the county." She spun to face him. "There's absolutely no bad."

Oh, there was bad. Lots of bad. Bad with a capital B. A. D. – as in Bloody Awful Disaster. He just couldn't explain it to her. The fact she believed it was a Christmas miracle was a miracle in and of itself, so he couldn't really expect another one to occur. Pity, because he hated to let her down but ... "It's just ... I like things how they are."

Her brow creased as confusion filled her eyes. "But Trip, don't you see, this could be the start of something big."

Oh, he saw. He saw more than she could ever know. He'd lived through people finding out a little too much about how the last 'miracle' he was responsible for had happened. There'd been excitement to begin with. And then there'd been pitchforks and torches and guns and the air filled with angry, frightened shouting and the acrid smell of thick smoke rising from his house, his pine trees and crops and orchards as they burned along with the field where it had happened.

While it was a few centuries on from that time, people hadn't changed that much. His Men in Black worries wouldn't be far from the truth and he would be subject to all sorts of horrible, invasive tests before he could say, "It's the magic of Christmas, not me!"

He took her hands in his. He had to stop her. "Please,

Daphne. I came here to live a quiet life. What you describe ... it makes me too uncomfortable. I don't want it."

"You don't want to bring joy to untold masses?"

He smiled crookedly at her. "Does it sound selfish to say no? No, I don't."

Her frown deepened. "You know, you don't have to hide yourself away like this. You have us now to protect you. And I know you love people – I see it every year at Christmas. Whatever happened in your past to make you live like a hermit for the rest of the year ... it doesn't need to touch you anymore."

He let go of her hands, stepped back. "I just ... I don't want it, okay?" She blinked, obviously startled by his stiff, firm tone. He didn't blame her – he never sounded so formal. But he couldn't help it right now. "Please, let's keep the miracle our secret."

She narrowed her eyes at him. "And how do you imagine we do that?"

"We don't tell anyone."

She sighed heavily. "You know the boys and I won't say a word if you don't want us to, but what about their friends? What about our neighbours? They're going to eventually see it. Not to mention we have the first of our Christmas tree bookings arriving this Saturday. You know a lot of them wander despite us telling them not to."

He chewed on his lip for a moment. "Well, given the people who've booked won't know that field was washed away a week ago, even if they happen upon it, they won't think there's anything miraculous about it." If they didn't look too closely and note all the plants that couldn't possibly have grown there.

She nodded reluctantly. "Okay, well, that might work for them, but what about our neighbours and the boys' friends? Cutter Thompson can see that field from his back paddock. And you know Gideon's friends often ride along the lane that runs beside that field when they're coming over to our place."

"We'll lock the gate to the lane, and your boys can tell their friends that I found toxic soil when I was clearing out the field and not to come down there. And in regard to Cutter … I guess we'll just have to hope he doesn't decide to suddenly put his cows in the back paddock. In the meantime, I'll get out there and trim it to try to make it look more normal." Although he'd have his work cut out for him. From experience, the things grown from his blood were pretty hardy. Even when he'd torn things out in the past, they grew back overnight. But he'd try.

She shook her head. "I don't understand why you're so against sharing something as wonderful as this. Particularly at this time of the year."

"I'm not asking you to understand. I'm just asking you to respect my wishes. Okay?"

Her mouth twitched from one side to the other, and for a moment he thought she was going to argue with him some more, but then she nodded. "Okay." She waved abruptly at the box that held the inflatable. "You better get on with erecting that, otherwise the Winter Wonderland won't be finished by Saturday."

He blushed at the overt reminder of what he'd actually been erecting when she'd burst in. "I will. Thank you."

She shrugged. "Don't thank me. I've not given up yet."

He chuckled. "I didn't expect you would. But I'm not going to change my mind."

"We'll see." She gave him a salute – their little joke because she'd always called him the captain of this mad little ship they called Snowy Hills Christmas Tree Farm.

He did fully intend on inflating the Santa and his rein-deers, but as he went to pull it out of its box, the whispers of the daydream came back to him, enticing him like a siren song.

He shook himself, shoving the images away. He had work to do. He couldn't keep giving in to the pull of the daydream and the need that tightened his balls every time he even thought about the woman and the way she'd looked at him. It was ridiculous really, the randy-teenager-esque bent of his thoughts. In reality, it hadn't happened like that. He'd been in pain and shocked then worried. And so confused.

Not really sexy at all.

Yet, his mind kept pushing him to go there with the memory of that moment.

He tried to ignore it, but it kept calling to him. Calling to him, and without realising, he was falling ... falling ...

EIGHT

The last week had been filled with nothing but frustration and false leads. The reference book had sent Ilia and the others to books that referred to events that were similar to what she'd seen Triptolemus do with his blood in that field. It was comforting to know she didn't have to worry about the evils of blood magic, but so frustrating to not find anything else.

There seemed to be nothing about what had happened after Demeter had removed his memory and taken much of his magic. Demeter's spell was effective in hiding him from everyone – including his own daughter. But they had to follow the leads even if they were centuries old, because they had nothing else.

Tamuel and Korinna went rushing off to check out the leads. They visited old churches, libraries and places of power across Europe and North and South America in search of more information. But they discovered no clues as to where Triptolemus might be now.

The desperation and hopelessness in Korinna's eyes every time they came back with nothing made something inside Ilia ache. She found herself rubbing her hand over where the HBG was embedded in her chest, blaming the ache on Clodia shifting and pounding at her prison in the gem even though she knew that wasn't it.

This was about the glow that kept appearing, the sensation like a small burn, growing larger and hotter with every false lead, every distraught expression Korinna tried to hide. It was made even worse by the fact she was hiding knowledge of that entry about Triptolemus and his line being God Killers and how that possibly tied her to them. She wished she could tell them because, while it might not help find him, it would give Korinna some clarity about why this had happened.

But she couldn't. The consequences would make things so much more complicated and difficult for her with what she must do in the future. And ultimately, it would hurt them all more than her hiding it from them would. What they didn't know couldn't hurt them, right?

The only thing she could do was to go back into the dream-vision over and over, trying to see something that might give her a clue as to where Triptolemus was now. But she found no new information or anything that might lead to some. The only thing that going back into her memory of her astral trip to him did was to fill her with an itchy longing every time she remembered how he'd looked knelt on the ground staring at her with those gorgeous eyes; eyes that made the cold she'd built up around her heart melt.

If that wasn't bad enough, she itched to touch his face, to brush over the bristles of his beard – hardly more than a few-days' worth of growth. She longed to brush her thumb over his plump lower lip, then follow with her lips. At least, that's what she'd done in her dreams every night since, and multiple times when in moments of despair she allowed herself to sink into daydreams that echoed the vision, but were hotter. Sexier.

Far sexier.

It actually infuriated her, the fact she kept losing herself to those stupid, hot daydreams. She wasn't some randy teenager. She was thousands of years old. At least, her spirit was. This body was only eight months old in a corporeal sense.

But that was neither here nor there.

She had learned long ago how disastrous giving in to hormonal lust was. Everything that had gone wrong in her life could be blamed on the fact she'd fallen head-over-heels in lust – she'd stupidly thought it love – with Mars and in doing so, set off a cascade of actions that had started with her father taking her boys from her and casting her, and them, away because of his fear, and bringing her and her mysterious witch heritage to the attention of Tiberinus.

So, these useless, stupid, tempting feelings she was experiencing weren't going to go anywhere or help with anything. She had to ignore them.

But, by the damned Gods, it was getting harder and harder as each day passed, and she didn't know why.

The only good thing about spending so much time in the library was that she didn't have to participate in any of Jules' Christmas plans – cookie and cake baking, painting new Christmas baubles for the various trees around the house, an endless viewing of every Christmas movie on all of the streaming services, and the constant singing of carols that were played non-stop during the day, piped through speakers that seemed to have appeared in all main rooms of the house.

Every morning, Ilia turned on stealth mode, getting up super early to race from her room to the kitchen to make her coffee and grab a piece of toast, and then race down into the library as quickly as she could before Jules or anyone else made it downstairs. And when they came down to the library, any time Jules or any of the others started to mention Christmas and family and tradition, she mysteriously had something to look up in the stacks and rushed off.

But waking morning after morning frustrated from sexilicious dreams, which really didn't help with quality sleep, was exerting a toll.

A week after she'd had the astral vision of Triptolemus using his blood to grow things, she woke, more tired than before. The struggle to pull her mind out of the sensual fog the too-hot dream created meant she stayed in bed long after her alarm went off. Then she spent longer in the shower than she meant to, trying to wake herself up – and trying to get rid of some of the sexual frustration with a bit of self-help. The end result of this was that when she made it downstairs to the kitchen, Jules was already there with Dawn, getting breakfast. Bas was there too, helping. Both looked up as she entered, smiling.

"Good morning," Jules sing-songed.

"Is it?"

Dawn, who was in her father's arms, cooed and did her grippy hand-wave thing, her smile bright as her dad placed her in her highchair. "Someone is a bit slug-a-bed this morning," Bas said, his voice low and rumbly.

She waved at Dawn, somehow managing a smile for the baby before turning to the coffee machine. "Just need coffee," she mumbled, trying to ignore the chirpy Christmas carols ringing through the kitchen from the speaker that unfortunately sat over her favourite kitchen appliance.

"I made cinnamon scrolls," Jules said, pointing at the table. "Help yourself. That is, of course, if those two have left any."

It was then she noticed Tamuel and Korinna sitting in the breakfast nook, sharing a kiss, a plate full of cinnamon scrolls before them.

"Looks like they haven't got to them yet," she said, turning away from the sight. Just in time to see Bas lean in to give Jules a kiss, his hands cupping her face in a way that spoke of love and adoration.

Hells.

She was in couples purgatory. Their loved-up antics were another reason she really didn't want to participate in all the Christmas goings on. Or keep hanging around like some sad third wheel after she'd separated herself from Dawn.

Seeing them and their happiness made her feel like shit. Not because she begrudged them their felicity, but because of the jealousy that speared through her every time she saw couples being all coupley.

That was when she noticed the coffee machine hadn't been turned on. Crap. It would take at least fifteen minutes to warm up to a point where she could make a decent coffee. She flicked the button on, dithering. She really didn't want to stay in the kitchen with the loved-up couples and happy family going on all around her while Christmas assaulted her every which way she looked, but she needed her coffee.

Shit. She couldn't even go to the cafe a few blocks away to get one because it was too far from Dawn. Maybe she could take Dawn for a walk?

She glanced back, trying to avoid seeing Jules and Bas, who were still kissing. By the looks of things, Dawn hadn't had her breakfast, which meant there was no chance she could take her for a walk.

Shit-crappity-fuck! She turned back to the coffee machine, staring at it, wishing it would hurry up. She snorted, knowing it was a ridiculous thing to do. Wishing for things had never got her anywhere.

She almost felt like crying. She just wanted her Gods-damned coffee and to disappear down into the library.

Rage began to simmer in her chest, the glow starting to shine.

Fuck!

She snapped her arms around herself to try and hide it. She couldn't let the others see – they'd ask questions and get worried and would want to help and they already had too much going on to waste time on some stupid glowy power that kept emanating from her chest when she couldn't control her emotions.

She had to get out of here. She turned to leave, and almost bumped into Jules. She hadn't even noticed the other witch coming up behind her.

"Ouch!" Jules said, shaking her hand. Then eyes widening, she said, "Ilia. Your chest!"

Crap! The rage was swept away in a rush of panic. The glow went along with it.

"Are you okay?"

"I ... I'm fine." She looked past Jules, thankful everyone else was too busy to notice what was happening.

"Is that the HBG doing that?"

Hells. She wished it was. It would be simpler to admit to that than the truth. She couldn't outright lie to Jules though – she was already lying every time she reported she'd found nothing new about Triptolemus – so she hedged by saying, "No. It just sometimes happens. Something to do with my body still trying to get used to Dawn's powers."

"Oh. But … it doesn't hurt?"

"No. As I said, I'm fine." She turned to leave.

"Ilia. Don't rush off, please. You've been working too hard – all of us have. So Bas and I have decreed this is a morning off for all of us. We're going to bake Christmas cookies for the neighbourhood party this weekend."

"We?"

Jules gestured behind her at the others in the kitchen. Tamuel and Korinna were still kissing. "Even grandmama is helping. When she gets back from the meeting with the Coven representatives overseeing the Yule celebrations."

A prickle started behind her eyes at the generosity of spirit that made Jules always want to include her. But … "I don't want to intrude on a family thing."

"Intrude? Why would you be intruding?"

Ilia waved at them all, her gesture taking in the kissing couple and Bas, who was now feeding Dawn her cereal. "You're all family and … I'm not. It doesn't feel right."

"But you are family. Of course you are."

She edged away a little, not liking the bright look in Jules' eyes. "No, I'm not. I'm just the unfortunate hanger-on you're stuck with for now because I'm magically attached to your daughter."

Jules sucked in a breath, her hand going out towards Ilia. Ilia stepped out of reach so the other witch's hand just hovered between them. "None of us think of you like that."

"I do." She looked away, unable to meet Jules' eyes, to see the slight trembling of her mouth. "You've all been so kind, but … I'm not your family. And you're not mine. My family died long ago. It's foolish to try to pretend otherwise."

"Do you truly feel like that?"

"I do." Without another word – and without her coffee – she turned and ran out of the kitchen. She'd not wanted to hurt the other witch, but she was horribly afraid she had. However, it was too late to take back what she'd said. Even if she apologised, it wouldn't undo the truth in her words.

She couldn't take that back, no matter how she tried.

More out of habit than anything else, she headed to the library, almost tripping down the stairs. It wasn't until she got to the bottom that she realised she'd been so upset, she hadn't raised her shields. She tried to do so now, but was too upset and the glow started up in her chest.

Shit. Shit.

She didn't know if the glow was the reason, but, despite the temptation of her without a shield, the library ghosts stayed away, as they'd been doing ever since she'd used her magic on them.

But what the Hells was she supposed to do about this glow? She couldn't work like this!

She stood there, sucking in deep breaths, trying to calm herself, to push the glow back inside. It took longer than it ever had before, but finally it faded and disappeared.

She blew out a breath. Hells, she needed a coffee now more than ever.

Trembling, she headed to the library's kitchenette and flipped the kettle on. There was no lovely coffee machine down here, but they did have instant coffee, which was nowhere as good but would do in a pinch if it was strong and sweet enough.

Then she'd turn her attention to trying to find where in the Hells Korinna's long-lost father was. Not only did she want to help Korinna, finding him was the only way she was going to be able to move on. And she seriously needed to do that – sooner rather than later.

She flicked the kettle on, got out a mug and added four heaped teaspoons of instant. And even though she would never usually sully a good coffee with sugar, she put in an equal number of teaspoons of sugar to balance out the bitterness.

As she put the sugar back on the shelf, there was a thump from the stacks just behind her.

She spun around, hands out, magic sparking on her fingertips, ready to fight off the ghosts. "Stupid, Ilia. You need to get your shields up."

But no ghosts appeared and the only sound she heard was a rustling coming from the Black Magic and Dangerous Books section.

She let out a trembling breath and lowered her hands. As she did, she noticed a book lying on the ground in front of the nearest stacks.

"Well, hello. You weren't there before."

She walked closer. There wasn't a gap in the shelves where it might have fallen from. So where had it come from? Had one of the ghosts dropped it there as an apology? But then, why not stick around so she knew?

Or was this another of the mysterious texts that just suddenly appeared here? Was this another piece of 'help' from Demeter?

Glancing up at the ceiling she said, "It better be helpful this time." Then slowly, carefully, she picked it up and turned it over.

The cover was dark green, the lettering on the front so faded she couldn't make it out. Magic buzzed in her fingertips; more magic than she'd previously felt in any of the books here, except for ones that were locked up.

"Shit." This wasn't something Demeter had found and brought to them. She knew well the feeling attached to this book. It was from the Black Magic and Dangerous Books section.

But how had it got out and landed here? The ghosts couldn't have brought it to her as they couldn't go inside that room. And it wasn't likely that Demeter would bring her a book of dark magic. So what had dropped it here for her to see?

Biting her lip, she wondered what she should do. Something was urging her to open it up, but that was a stupid thing to do without anyone else here to help if something went wrong. The last time a book had opened of its own accord from the lock up, it had taken both Korinna and Tamuel to capture the entity inside it and push it back in the book and lock it away. With her magic still being so unfamiliar, she was no match for whatever lay inside.

Gingerly, she placed it on the table. She had to go back upstairs and get Korinna and Tamuel at least. Hopefully she wouldn't walk in on more lovey-doviness, although there was nothing she could do to avoid the Christmas joy.

She rolled her eyes. She really wasn't in the mood, but did she have a choice?

She'd taken two steps when a wind whipped around her, pushing her back towards the table. She stumbled, turning to catch herself on the table's edge before she fell. "What the Hells?"

She tried to push upright but the wind didn't let up, curving around her like arms to keep her there no matter how much she struggled against it.

Before her, the cover of the book flipped open, the pages fluttering up and over. Then just as suddenly as it came, the wind was gone and the book stilled.

On the open page was a picture.

Of a face she recognised.

Underneath, the confirmation she needed. A name. Triptolemus.

Without meaning to, she reached out to touch the edge of his strong chin.

And fell into a vision.

The world swung around Ilia as she fell. Bile rose in her throat. Her heart beat fast and hard in her chest; her breath was a tight pain that couldn't seem to get out, not even in a scream.

She closed her eyes. Then, as quickly as it had started, the falling, spinning stopped.

There was no jolt as she steadied, although she appeared to be standing upright. On a firm surface.

She opened her eyes.

And there he was – the man she now knew to be Triptolemus.

He stood before her, much as he'd been when she'd first seen him in the vision.

Except this time, he wasn't injured and he *was* standing.

To full attention.

In every sense of the word.

A fact she immediately noticed because he was stark naked. Every single inch of his tanned and muscled body on full and delicious display.

If that wasn't hot enough, he smiled, a sexy smile that

touched her in all the right places. A smile that was more wicked and enticing than anything she'd ever seen.

In fact, she felt that smile in every nerve and sinew in a way she'd never experienced before, even with Mars. And it was overwhelming.

Heat flared over her, through her and there was a sudden flood of wetness right in that most sex-starved part of her.

Gods, he was sex on a stick. Just plain lickable.

She wanted to fan herself but didn't seem to have control over her limbs. In fact, all she seemed capable of right now was to stare at him, every part of her unbearably itchy and hot and needy.

So needy.

His smile widened as his gaze roved over her, hunger flaring in his eyes. And amusement. "You're dressed differently this time."

"This time?"

He gestured at her, his cock flexing. "No Roman gown with clips." He touched his shoulder and suddenly all she wanted to do was run her hand over that firm breadth of skin and feel the warm silk of it, the strength of muscle beneath. And lick it.

See. Definitely lickable.

She roped her wandering thoughts back in, forcing herself to concentrate on this strange conversation, so unlike any she'd had in previous dreams. "I'm all out of Roman gowns with clips."

"Pity. I did like how they ... draped."

Yea Gods! That pause.

It did things to her insides that shouldn't be possible. But that pause brought to mind all the dreams she'd had lately of her undoing clips on a gown she barely took notice of as she reached for him, baring herself to him as he was bared to her now. "They did … drape nicely."

"Hmm. I think I almost prefer this though." His smile widened even further and he waggled his brows at her. "Do they flop when you walk?"

What? Then she noticed his gaze had dropped to her feet. Hers followed and she almost groaned.

Bunny slippers!

Why was she wearing bunny slippers in this vision? Sure, she had slipped them on this morning after tugging on her shorts and t-shirt before dragging herself downstairs and enduring that disastrous conversation in the kitchen. But never before had she worn her actual clothes in a vision. She'd always been draped in something distinctly closer to what she'd worn when she'd been alive the first time.

But this time, it was green shorts, a bright pink t-shirt and her purple bunny slippers.

Sexy … not!

She shifted. The ears flopped around.

Triptolemus chuckled.

Her knees wobbled at the husky wisp of sound. It wrapped around her, vibrated through her, caressed every erogenous zone on the way, leaving her tingling and even more needy.

"I never knew how sexy bunnies could be," Triptolemus said, voice still a low, aching rasp that made her nerves tremble and her nipples peak so hard she was certain they were very visible now through bra and t-shirt.

"Sexy?"

"Oh Gods yes. And who knew I was a leg man?"

She stared down – thank everything holy she'd shaved

her legs that morning in the shower. "You are?" This was the strangest vision.

"Oh yes. Prior to this, I would have said I was all about your breasts, but looking at your legs in those short little shorts, capped off with those bunny slippers ..." He licked his lips. "Oh Hells yes. I'm a leg man."

Her gaze went to his legs – thick, muscled thighs and defined calves dusted with dark hair over sun-kissed skin, narrow ankles, large shapely feet. "I find I'm rather partial to legs too." Her gaze roved back up, arrowing in on his thick erection. "I'm also rather partial to other things."

His erection flexed, brushing against the six-pack he sported. "All hail other things! I have to admit, this 'other thing' is rather partial to 'other things' as well."

Her gaze flew up to find his roving over her once again, finally coming to meet her eyes.

The impact stole her breath.

"You have the most extraordinary eyes. They're like the velvet dark of night kissed by the dawn."

Oh! What a thing to say. Her heart squeezed and warmed in a way that felt like she was melting. In a good way. In the best way.

"And your hair? It's been dawn-touched too. Like the rays of sun whispering over the hills, lighting the sky with gold and lilac and peach. And so silky-looking, I just want to wrap my hands in it and find out if it feels as soft as it looks. If it's cool or warm."

Her heart did that thing again, squeezing and warming in a way that would have worried her if not for the fact that other things were squeezing and warming. She never knew words could be so sexually powerful. She swallowed hard, touched her hair, fingers sliding through the lock falling over her shoulder. "I was going to cut it short."

"Oh no. Never do that. It's perfect the way it is. Glorious. In fact, it shines like a halo in the sun. You're like an angel. My Christmas angel."

"Pfft." She waved away the idea. "I'm simply a woman."

He let out an unsteady breath. "Nothing simple about you." He took in another breath, his muscled chest expanding, his tanned skin glowing in the strange light of this place. "Did you know you glow?"

Her lips twitched. "You're a poet and you don't know it?"

He laughed, the sound a brilliant burst around her, doing much the same as his chuckle had done earlier. She wanted to wrap herself in that laugh, in the warmth and joy of it.

In her long, long life, that kind of joy and warmth had been non-existent.

His laughter died when she didn't join him, didn't even smile. His gaze met hers again, the hunger intensifying in the depths of his brilliant, spring-green eyes. "I'm serious. You actually glow."

"It's the light of this place." She gestured around them at the garden they were in. The garden he'd created with his blood. "It's different here. You're glowing too."

He looked down at himself, raising his arms, turning them over. "No. My skin is simply reflecting the light. The glow in you comes from within. I noticed it the first time I saw you. And every time since."

Every time since?

Was he talking about the dreams? But that wasn't possible. They'd been her dreams. Not visions. Not astral travel or whatever this was. Just hot, wet, sexy dreams – more fantasy than dream – that she couldn't seem to shake no matter how much she tried.

So, how had he seen them too?

She wanted to ask, but he got in first by asking, "So, my Christmas angel, do you have a name?"

"Ilia."

His brow quirked. "Ilia." He said her name like he was breathing it in, tasting it, and the sensation pleased him. "So, Ilia. How is it you glow if you're not an angel?"

"I was brought into this life with an ancient spell at dawn with magic that was Goddess-given by Ostara." She had no idea why she'd told him that, but the words just tumbled out.

He nodded. "Makes sense. The first time I saw you it was like I saw the sun's rays at dawn after being stuck in the dark all my life."

Again with the words. He was good with the words.

Damn him.

It was doing something to her that she didn't think she liked, but was powerless to stop. Especially given he wasn't using his looks and magnetism to pull her in like most males – God or man – would. Okay, he was standing there completely starkers, but he'd done nothing to take advantage of that fact. He'd just used humour and bantering and the loveliest compliments she'd ever been given.

And boy, it was working. Not that it needed to work. She'd been ready to jump his bones the moment she'd seen him; she didn't need anything else.

Yet ... instead of moving towards him, she asked, "What's going on here?"

He glanced down at himself then looked up at her through his eyelashes. "A baring of souls?"

She snort-laughed, slapping her hand to her lips, mortified. She'd never made that sound in her long existence.

He laughed too, plush lips splitting wide, white teeth

flashing, head tipping back, the laugh vibrating in his chest and throat. Such a laugh, it made her laugh with him. At him. At her. At this strange situation they were in.

Slowly, their laughter petered out. He took a slow step towards her, head tipped to the side. "What brought you here?"

TEN

Ilia blinked. What had brought her here?

Ah, yes. "A book. There was an image of you. I touched it and then here I was." She tipped her head to the side. "You?"

"I think maybe you brought me here."

"What do you mean?"

"I was about to get on with my day after ..." He stopped, cheeks flushing and waved his hand. "Never mind. It's a long story. Needless to say, I was finally determined to stop getting sucked into the wet-daydreams when bam! I was sucked into this. I assume it was you who brought me here."

"I didn't mean to." She frowned. "Although, if it was me, why would I bring you here with no clothes on? I mean, I'm wearing the clothes I had on before coming here. Unless you weren't dressed when dragged here?"

"No, I was dressed." He raised a brow. "Maybe this is how you want to see me."

Heat rushed up her chest and into her face. He was right. She'd been imagining what he looked like after every non-fulfilling dream ended with her disrobing and him staying clothed, then disappearing before they'd even got to touch. She should lie about that, but … "Maybe. Or maybe it's about time that you're the one who's naked."

"All's fair," he said. "In love and war?"

Love? Why did panic rise in her chest at that word? To cover, she snorted and said, "Love. That's hardly applicable to these dreams of ours. That's just lust."

"Is it? Is it only that? When you appear and look at me like that, it feels deeper than lust. It feels—"

"Whoa! Hold that thought right there, Mister. We don't know each other."

He looked down at himself then back at her. One brow cocked. "Really."

Heat rushed over her again. Almost against her will, she took a stumbling step towards him before managing to stop herself from rushing to him, giving more away than she was willing to. He had to meet her part way.

But he didn't move. Every part of him was tensed, as if waiting for something. She wasn't certain what, given the look in his eyes.

She licked her lips. He raised his brow, his erection twitching against his stomach.

"So?"

"So."

She might have wanted the words before, but now, she wanted more. Needed more. "Are you going to continue to talk, or are you going to come over here?" She had no idea where those words came from either – her one and only time spent with any male in this way had been nothing like this. She'd not been this bold, this forward. She'd completely followed Mars' lead. He'd taken. She'd given. And thought that was love.

So stupid.

But she wasn't stupid now. She knew this wasn't love, despite Triptolemus' inference that more was going on between them. For her, it was lust. Pure and simple. Not that lust was either pure or simple. But whatever.

Looking at him filled her with lust.

And by the evidence before her, looking at her filled him with the same. But still, he didn't move. "Please," she managed to say.

"Please what?" he asked, that smile widening a little more.

"Please. I need you. Now."

"Now?"

"Yes, now!"

"So demanding. Why are you always so demanding?"

"Because you like it that way."

"Do I?"

"Oh yes, you do."

She was shocked at herself but also delighted. It was freeing, this open, teasing talk. And so damned hot, especially with that look flaring in his eyes that mirrored the sensations firing through her.

And yet, he held back, sucking in an unsteady breath. "Oh, Ilia. I would like nothing more than to come over there and explore this. But given we seem more in control of things this time, shall we try to figure out why we keep being drawn back to each other? Or even why this is happening in the first place?"

Sexual heat fizzled inside her. She'd never been more disappointed in all her life, but Hells. He was right. Given this chance, she couldn't let the others down. "I know why. We've been looking for you."

"We?"

She nodded. "And then I found you when I astrally projected to you. I think the quality in your blood that allowed you to grow those plants brought me to you, allowed us to talk briefly. But there wasn't enough information."

"Information? About me?"

"That. And where you are."

He glanced around him. "On my farm."

"Yes, but where?"

"Why do you need to find me?"

She paused. Was that really her news to tell? Not really. "Don't you want me to?"

His gaze heated once more as it raked over her from head to toe and back again. "Oh yes. I really want to. I want to see you in the flesh. I want to feel your skin under mine, not just reach for it and have you disappear. I want you here with me."

"I want that too."

"Good. Because I can't get you out of my thoughts. I don't think I even want to."

She couldn't get him out of her thoughts either. Although, she really wanted to. After this lust was slaked, she'd be able to. "Well?"

"Well what?"

"Where are you?"

"I'm—"

"Ilia? Ilia? Are you okay? Ilia?"

The words thundered around her, covering his answer, and before she could figure out what was happening, she was whisked away. "No!" she screamed.

She came back to herself with a thud and a horrible sense that she'd just wasted her one and only chance to get the information they needed. "No, no, no!" She slammed her hands back on the picture of Triptolemus, running her fingers over his face. "Take me back! Take me back! I'm not finished. I'm not finished!"

"Ilia!"

"She's hysterical."

"She's still lost in the vision."

Bas, Tamuel and Korinna stood around her. They must have pulled her out of the vision. But they didn't understand. She had to get back. To him. She had to find out where he was. Then she had to jump his bones. She hadn't got to jump his bones.

Her skin felt like a live-wire was attached. Her nerves jumping. Heat flashed through her. Power sparked on her fingertips, in her chest. She began to fall again.

"Look at her chest! It's glowing."

"The gem. It must be Clodia doing this."

"No. Wrong colour. This is something else. We need to make her let go of that book."

Hands grabbed her arms, others wound around her waist. They pulled at her.

Her grip on the book began to slip, fingers raking across the page, across that incredibly handsome face. She scrabbled to hold on, getting her clawed fingers around the edge of the book.

"Ilia, you've got to let go."

"No! No. Don't make me stop. I almost had it. Don't make me stop!"

"Ilia. It's taking your life's energy. It's affecting Dawn."

Those words. They got through.

Her grip slipped.

The arms around her, holding her shoulders, her waist, pulled and they lurched back.

And he was truly gone. "No, no, no! I didn't find him! I didn't find him!" Tears tumbled down her face.

"Find who?" Tamuel asked, his voice close to her ear – he was holding her up.

"By the Heavens. Look at that!" Korinna exclaimed.

"What?" Bas asked from Ilia's other side. He was holding her too?

"It's my father."

"Words are appearing."

They were?

She looked down and sure enough, words appeared across the bottom of the picture that had taken her into the vision with Triptolemus.

"Find me at Snowy Hills Christmas Tree Farm, Tasmania."

"Does that mean what I think it means?" Korinna asked, her voice wobbling.

"Ilia?"

She blinked, staring at the words. "Y-yes. I saw him. He was about to tell me where he was when you pulled me out. I don't know how, but he managed to tell me even though you ripped me away."

"We had to, Ilia. The book was killing you. And Dawn. It sucks on your soul's energy to power the visions it gifts. That's why it's locked away and has a warning attached for anyone who wants to use it."

Did it? She hadn't seen any warning.

"Why did you bring it out here and use it without one of us with you?" Tamuel asked.

"I didn't. It just appeared. Like those other texts appeared."

"It what?" Korinna looked at Tamuel and Bas, her eyes wide. "That's not possible."

Bas shook his head slowly. "No, it's not. The only way a book can get out of the Black Magic and Dangerous Books section is if someone takes it out."

"Or lets it out," Tamuel said ominously. "We never got to the bottom of who let the book out Korinna and I battled before Easter."

"We've been a bit busy," Korinna said. "Besides, its release helped us to find the solution to how we could blend our magic together and let Ilia out of the HBG, so it felt like the intent behind that was positive. And I have to say, this feels the same. If that book hadn't been let out for Ilia to use, we'd never have discovered where to find my father."

"You don't think it could be a trap?"

Korinna took Tamuel's hand. "This is the best lead we've had. We have to follow it."

"True," Bas said. "But you need to be careful. Whoever put this information before us like this is playing a dangerous game. Ilia and Dawn could have been seriously hurt – or killed – if we hadn't found her before it went too far." He turned to her. "Ilia, are you okay?"

She opened her mouth to answer, but her legs suddenly gave out. Thankfully Bas caught her. "I think I need to sit down," she said weakly.

"Here." He picked her up and walked to the couch where he lowered her gently so she was lying down.

It should have been a relief, but her head ached and her breathing was a little too slow and hard.

"Oh Gods. Ilia. What can we do?" Tamuel asked as Korinna knelt beside her and took her hand.

"Nothing. I'll take care of her," Bas said. "You and Korinna need to check out the address in the book, Tam."

"Are you sure?" Korinna asked, her voice wavering with

worry and excitement as her hands clenched on Ilia's. "Jules might need help with Dawn, and you with Ilia. Checking to see if my father's at that address can wait."

"No, it can't," Tamuel said grimly. "You're having more intense nightmares every night, Rinna. You know the darkness is drawing near. We need to find Triptolemus sooner rather than later."

"But ... Ilia. Dawn. How can we go when they're like this?"

"Because Tam is right," Ilia managed to say, removing her hands from Korinna's grip and patting her arm. "I'll be fine."

Bas nodded. "We'll be able to handle this. They both should recover quickly now Ilia is no longer in contact with the book."

"Really?" Korinna's gaze bored into her, her eyes filled with hope and worry.

"Really. You need to go. Now." How could saying so few words sap her of all energy? But she held herself together because Korinna wouldn't go otherwise.

"See. They'll both be fine." Bas raised his brow at Ilia and he smiled, grateful, before his gaze went to Tam. "But just be careful, my son. Okay?"

"Of course. We don't know if that message is from Triptolemus or from something else entirely."

"We'll be careful," Korinna promised as she got to her feet and took Tamuel's hand.

Portal magic prickled the air in front of the couch but Ilia didn't see them step through because blackness surrounded her and she passed out.

ELEVEN

Trip slammed out of the vision as fast as he was sucked into it. He fell back on his couch with a thump. Breath exploded out of him.

"Shit!" He grasped at his chest, fingers clenching on his t-shirt as he struggled to breathe. His cock pressed hard against his shorts, still at attention despite his inability to catch his breath.

And in his mind, her face as clear as day.

Ilia.

He knew her name now!

Ilia.

It suited her, the name like sunlight shining from beyond a mountain, lighting the sky.

He smiled sappily, sinking softly into the couch, his hand going to his crotch and …

"Shit-crap-fuck!" He leaped to his feet, shoving his hands behind him. It had almost happened again. What in all the Hells was wrong with him? He'd never acted like this. Ever. And the fact Daphne had caught him masturbating last week and yet he was still at it like some horny teenager …

Something else was manipulating him. He was certain of it.

But why?

He stared around his lounge room as if to find the answers there. When nothing came, he blew out a long breath, raking his hands through his hair.

Was this happening because they were meant to be together? That might explain the outrageous lust and also the deeper feeling that he knew her somehow. Was this the Fates' way of making up for the crappy hand he'd been dealt? Maybe. Although, she didn't seem too keen on that idea when he'd tried to bring it up. All she'd seemed to want was his body … and for some strange reason, his address.

'We've been looking for you.' Those were her words. Who was the mysterious 'we' and why did they want to find him?

A crawling sensation prickled over his skin. Maybe he shouldn't have shouted his address out to her when she abruptly flew up and away from him.

Had she heard him?

Was she coming to find him? Would she just appear, like the best, most sexy Christmas gift he'd ever seen? Or would she be with the 'we'?

The front doorbell rang, making him jump.

He sucked in a breath. Could that be …?

He stumbled to the door as if in a dream. The doorbell peeled again just as he got there. He smiled. She was just as impatient to see him as he was to see her. He pulled the door open with such force it was a miracle it didn't tear off its hinges. "Thank the Gods you heard me. I—"

He stared at the handsome couple who stood on his front veranda. A man and a woman. He didn't really notice anything about the man because his attention was drawn to the woman. Not Ilia, but equally as mesmerising in a very different way. She stared at him with eyes that were the exact same colour as his. He'd never seen eyes that colour, other than when he looked in the mirror. "What ...? Who are you?"

"Triptolemus?"

That name ... Ilia had called him that. And like it had then, it made him feel a little sick as a bell clanged through his head over and over in time to the syllables. He winced and pressed his palm against his forehead where pain throbbed along with the clanging.

"Oh my Goddess, it's you! I can't believe we've finally found you!"

Found him? Were they Ilia's 'we'? And why wasn't she here with them? She was supposed to be here too. He felt it deep in his soul. "This ... isn't ... right," he managed to say around the pounding in his head.

"Triptolemus? Are you alright? Triptolemus?"

Hells. The pain in his head got worse every time the woman said his name. "I'm not Triptolem ... Triptol ... Tripto—" The pain threatened to fell him when he tried to say the name, so he stopped and said, "My name's Trip. Trip O'Dem." The name had been the only thing left to him when he'd woken all those years ago – that and the bags of gold – and as he said it, the pain slipped away.

"Trip." Her lips wobbled. "I like it."

He frowned. What did it matter if she liked his name? And yet, it did. And why was there something so familiar about her? The familiarity wasn't just in the fact they shared the same colour eyes. It was something else he couldn't put his finger on, yet he was certain he'd never seen her before in this life.

He cleared his throat. "Who are you?"

The woman's hand went to her throat. "Do you not recognise me? They say I look like my mother."

He stared at her, his chest tightening.

Her mother? Had he known her mother? Maybe that's why she looked familiar. For a glimmering moment, a wisp of memory of a face very like hers shimmered in his mind's-eye before a stabbing pain sent it spiralling away.

Biting back another wince, he said, "I ... I've never seen you before. And I have no idea who your mother is."

"Oh, I ..." She swallowed hard, her upset obvious.

His chest ached. He wanted to touch her face, to tell her everything would be okay.

But she was a stranger. A stranger who might know Ilia.

For some reason though, he couldn't come out and just ask. Her name seemed locked in his throat. Instead, he asked, "Who are you?"

"I'm Korinna Soteira. This is my mat— My husband, Tamuel Stevens."

He shook his head. The names held an echo, like something long forgotten, but he was certain he'd never heard them before. "Doesn't ring a bell. Why do you think I'm supposed to know you?" The longer this conversation went on, the more he was coming to think they had nothing to do with Ilia. Because if they did, wouldn't they mention her?

"I ... I suppose it was foolish to hope you would." The woman blinked rapidly, her gaze flickering to the man she'd identified as Tamuel. He didn't say anything, just took her hand in his, holding it tight, and for a moment, Trip could have sworn that his dark eyes glowed violet as he met Korinna's gaze.

Power pulsed from both of them.

These people were not human. At least, not fully. He took a step back, panic a tight grip in his chest. Something inside him told him to run, that he could never let himself be caught by anyone else with magic.

Except, he hadn't felt that with Ilia. And she most definitely had magic.

This must be proof that these people had nothing to do with her.

He took a step back, reaching for the door. "I don't know what your business is here, but I want you to go."

The woman stepped forward, hands clasped together, eyes beseeching. "Please, don't. I've come a long way to meet you. There's things … things I have to say. Things you need to know."

"I need to know nothing from you."

He went to close the door, but the man – Tamuel – waved his hand and the door sprang out of Trip's hand to slam back against the wall. "Please. Triptolemus. You need to listen."

Anger welled inside him, burning away the panic and fear that their presence brought, and the pain the sound of that name evinced. He gripped the door and yanked it from its position against the wall. It wasn't easy to move, but he gritted his jaw and pulled until he slammed it in their faces.

The last thing he saw was the surprised expression on the man's face and tears in the woman's eyes.

Arms and legs trembling, he leaned back against the door.

"Well, that didn't go well," he heard the man say through the door.

"It's him. She found him. I can't believe it's really him."

"It is wonderful, my heart, but I don't think he was lying when he didn't seem to remember anything about you at all."

"I know. I have to admit that I thought if he just saw me it would break the spell."

"I hoped that too but ... did you see the fear in his eyes? That doesn't bode well for making him listen to us."

"It must have something to do with the spell Demeter put on him to take his memories and keep him safe."

At the sound of that name – Demeter – Trip's legs gave way and he slid to the floor, the room swaying and swirling around him. Even so, the couple's conversation came through the door loud and clear, piercing the fog in his mind.

"But how am I to get through to him? I need him to listen. I need him to teach me about my birthright and to explain exactly why he did what he did."

"Maybe Ilia can help. She's the one who's been seeing him."

Ilia! They did know Ilia. They were her 'we'!

He tried to move, but his limbs were just too sluggish and his head too full of pain as their words swirled around him.

"Yes. But ... if she comes, it means everyone has to come and they'll have to come by plane then drive because Dawn gets too sick going through the portal. And how can I ask Jules to leave right now with all her Christmas plans in place?"

"I don't think we have a choice. He obviously still has some of his power – did you see how he moved the door despite me holding it with my power? Not to mention what helped us to find him. Ilia's dreams then that vision and now the book!"

"And what about the thing Ilia says he did with his blood? Growing the plants in that field. Do you think his blood is what drew her in some way, because of what we did at Easter with my blood and yours, mixing them with the power of the ring and the power of Oestra?"

"I don't know. It's possible."

"But what does it mean?"

"I can't answer that. What I *am* concerned about is if the media gets wind of the miracle Garden of Eden growing in his paddock, they'll have a field day. It might even get so big an issue it could draw Zeus and the other Gods' attention – and we don't want any of them turning this way before we've discovered how to get his memories back."

"I'm sure there's things we can do to stop that from happening."

"True. You should try using your powers with your ring. If he grew all that from his blood, I'm sure yours mixed with the gem can help undo it all so it doesn't seem so ... miraculous."

Trip held his breath as their words punched through his spinning thoughts. Could they take care of that problem for him? Perhaps he should go out, talk to them, ask for the help they seemed so ready to give. Especially given they did know Ilia. Were talking about bringing her down here.

Ilia.

Every time they said her name, it pushed aside the pain and confusion, the sound of it a burst of brightness in his mind like the most perfect of blooms, carrying her perfumed scent along with it, like night-blooming jasmine and roses as they were warmed by the sun's rays at dawn.

Ilia.

"She is the one. The one who will save you. You must get her here. You must drink of her blood."

The thought jagged in his mind, stopping him from spinning back into the wet-daydream again. He tried once more to get up, but his limbs were like jelly and he slid back to the floor.

The voices outside grasped his attention.

"... using your powers isn't what's worrying you, is it?" Tamuel was saying.

Korinna snorted. "Hardly. I'm feeling much more on top of them now. The Eleusinian Mysteries Grimoire has helped so much with that."

The what? Those words, they sounded like he should know them. No ... like he *did* know them.

"I've still got so much to learn. There's so much I don't know. I mean, how did he do it? How did he grow things with just his blood? I didn't think we were supposed to be able to do any of that without the ring because of how our blood is cursed. I didn't see him wearing it on his hand."

The ring?

A vision of a ring, thick gold with a green gem set in it, appeared in his mind's eye. He'd had that ring on his finger when he'd woken, but he'd taken it off and hidden it before walking into the first village he'd come across. For some reason, he'd kept it hidden ever since.

So how did they know about the ring? He wanted to ask, but still couldn't seem to stand, or make a sound. All he could do was listen.

"... I don't know. Maybe Demeter took it before she wiped his mind."

He clutched his head as pain spiked through it again. That name. Pain came every time they said it.

"I can't believe she's disappeared. I thought now that

I'd discovered all she'd hidden from me, she'd speak about it at last and tell me why."

"Does Persephone know where she's gone yet?"

Persephone. More pain in his head; but not as bad as the ache in his heart at the sound of that name.

"No. She has no clue. Seph is really worried. And she can't tell me anything either because she's bound by the vows she made to her mother. All we have is what Ilia heard Demeter say when she was in possession of the HBG."

"Well, we've got no choice. We have to ask everyone to come down here. Before he does something more to out himself than he's already done. Given Ilia is certain he's seen her in the dream-vision, he might listen to her."

Ilia? They would bring her here? He pushed past the pulsing pain and listened harder.

"First, we should go and deal with that field."

"Yes. Let's do that. Then we need to call Jules so she can organise flights to get them all down here."

"You don't want to go back and tell them?"

"No. I can't leave him. I want to stay close." Thick tears in the woman's voice. "I didn't think meeting my father would be like this."

Father? The word rang through his mind, stealing his breath, drowning out the sound of the male's reply.

She couldn't mean that word in relation to him. He was nobody's father. He hadn't made his vow to not get involved with a woman lightly. It was too dangerous, not only because he couldn't risk anyone finding out the truth about him, but because he couldn't risk passing on to a child his cursed blood, as she called it. And she was right. For surely it was a curse when he had to hide it from the world for fear of what would happen if the truth got out. Look what had happened with the small amount he'd spilled in his field, and the trouble that waited in the wings because of it.

These people obviously knew all about it. Perhaps they could get rid of the curse.

The thought brought energy to his limbs with a sudden rush, enabling him finally to push to his feet. He was still wobbly and it took a few moments of him leaning against the door to get his breath back.

There was a rush over his skin, akin to the lightning pricks of static electricity, and a gust of wind blew under the door.

What in the Hells? He managed to right himself long enough to pull the door open.

They were gone, dirt and leaves whirling in a spiral a foot above the ground in the place they'd just stood.

CHAPTER

TWELVE

"Damn!"

He swung around to make certain Daphne and her boys hadn't been around to see them disappear. Daphne wouldn't swallow a Christmas miracle again and neither would her boys.

But thankfully, there was no sign of them. They were either all working in the shop, getting it ready for Saturday, or preparing the tractors – Gideon had dressed them up like reindeers for last Saturday and there were some issues with antlers staying in place that the boys had been working on all week to delight their guests this weekend.

Would Korinna and Tamuel be back with Ilia and the other people they spoke of on Saturday? Could he wait until then? He supposed he had to. It wasn't like he knew where they were.

Although ... he did. They said they were going to take care of the magically grown garden.

Limbs still a little wobbly, he raced as fast as he could to where he'd parked his ute. He barely had the door shut before he'd started it and was off down the lane that led to the field. He swore at every gate he had to stop at and open, not bothering to close them behind him as he'd told Daphne and the boys they must – he'd get them on the way back. He needed to speak to this Korinna and Tamuel. And he had no idea how long they would be at their task. They were dealing with magic after all. If his blood could grow a lush garden in a few seconds, then it shouldn't take them much longer to get rid of it – should it? He really didn't know how any of this worked. Something else he had to learn from them.

Hells. Why had he acted like such an idiot? They'd appeared just after he'd shouted his address in the dream to Ilia. Of course she'd sent them. He should have trusted them. He blamed years of living alone and barely trusting anyone. Well, he had to trust them now. They had answers.

And Ilia.

As he drove closer, a glowing green light rose above the hill between him and the field.

Korinna's magic. She was already at it. Hells.

He pushed down on the accelerator, the revving engine complaining loudly. He didn't care. He had to get there.

The light glowed and pulsed. In the morning sun, it wasn't too bright, but what if people on nearby properties saw that glow and wondered what was going on? Shit. He hadn't thought of that. His magic didn't have a colour. Things just grew. This was something different.

He crested the rise that led down into the valley where the field was. His foot hit the break and he jerked forward at the abrupt stop.

Green light flowed from Korinna's right hand, reaching out to twine around and cover the plants he'd grown with his blood. The man she'd called her husband – Tamuel – stood at her side, a blue and purple glow growing around him, feeding down his arm and into the hand clasped around hers.

Was he feeding his power into her in some way? What for? A dual power? Was that a thing?

Once again, he had no idea.

But all those questions fled as the green glow fell on the garden he'd accidentally grown and started to press down. The plants began to disappear, turning into a fine green mist that settled on the ground. As it did, hundreds of pine tree seedlings, like what had been there before the storm, appeared.

The green power fluttered then withdrew with a snap into Korinna's ring.

The young witch who claimed he was her father – he shook his head at the impossible-to-fathom thought – seemed to sag a little. Tamuel held her up, arm around her waist, his magic still feeding into her.

She straightened, smiled up at her powerful husband, then kissed him gently on the lips.

He returned her kiss before pulling away to wave his hand, his power changing as it flew from his outstretched fingertips. The air in front of them wobbled, then began to spin, sparking with blue and purple lights. The air split and a round ... portal? He didn't know how he knew the word, but he was certain that was right ... spun there.

They were leaving!

He hit the accelerator and began to honk his horn, shouting out the window, "Don't go. Don't go!"

They turned.

Fearful they'd leave despite the fact they'd stopped and were staring at him as he drove madly towards them, he didn't bother getting out to open the gate, just crashed through it.

To their credit, they didn't move or try to run from the madman careering towards them in a ute.

He stopped the ute and jumped out. "The ring! You used the ring!" The words exploded out of his mouth on each pant of breath as he ran the last few metres to them.

She held out her hand, the ring and its green gem gleaming on the middle finger of her right hand. Exactly like his.

"You remember the ring?" she said as he came to a stop in front of her.

"I have one too."

She smiled slowly. "I know."

"I didn't know it could do that." He gestured at the field of Christmas tree seedlings.

"You weren't meant to know," Tamuel said.

"But you can tell me?" He couldn't look anywhere but at Korinna and the ring.

"We hoped you'd be able to tell us," Korinna said. "I'd hoped just seeing me would break the spell and make you remember."

He shook his head slowly, sadly. "I can't remember. I can't remember who I was before I woke up all those years ago. All I remember is this," he said, gesturing around him. "This life. And even that I struggle with. I have diaries, but there are so many by now, it's impossible to look over them, to keep up with everything I've lived through; everything I've done."

"Well, we're hoping we'll be able to help you with that."

"They will. They can help. But only after Ilia is here. Only after you have drunk her blood."

The voice rang in his mind, louder than it had ever been in any of his wet-daydreams or even when he'd seen Ilia in this field.

"The blood," he said. "It's all in the blood."

Korinna looked down at the ring, and he noticed for the first time the blood on her skin, sizzling on the gem. "Do you mean my blood? Or your blood?"

He shook his head. "*Her* blood. The one you call Ilia. You have to get her here. Her blood is the key."

"What? Why?" Her eyes were wide with shock and questions. So many questions. But she only asked one more. "How do you know that?"

"I ..." He shook his head, trying to clarify his thoughts. This had to make sense to them even though it didn't make sense to him. "A voice keeps telling me. I heard it first when she appeared in my field and then ..." he blushed a little, "... in dreams I've had ever since."

"Dreams? Tell me about the dreams."

His blush deepened. It was bad enough Daphne knew about his lascivious mind. If this woman was actually somehow his daughter, he most definitely didn't want her knowing how he lusted after her friend.

But, if he was to get their help, he needed to tell them something more than he had to convince them.

Taking a deep breath he said, "She is standing there, like she was that day, but in the dreams she's wearing this Grecian-type gown with gold butterfly clips on the shoulders." Not in the most recent one, of course, but he most definitely wasn't sharing that with them. It was too intimate. Too ... everything.

He cleared his throat and forced his mind back to the other dreams. "She reaches for me and tells me to drink of her blood, that it will make everything right. Except, come to think of it, it's not really her voice."

Korinna and Tamuel shared a look. "A Grecian gown? With butterfly clips?" They asked him together.

"That means something to you?"

"It's a message from Demeter," Korinna said. "It has to be."

Trip winced at the name.

They looked at him. "Are you okay?" Korinna asked, reaching to touch his arm.

He let her, wondering at how good it felt, how right. He stared at her.

"Trip?"

He suddenly remembered her question. "Yes, it's just, some of the names you say, they give me pain."

She glanced at Tamuel. "Part of the spell?"

"Makes sense. From what Ilia told us, your mentor wouldn't want him looking into anything that might lead him to the truth until you were ready."

"So, it's true then. Ilia's blood is somehow the key."

Tamuel was grim as he returned his attention to Trip. "It makes sense. Her magic was always special and incredibly strong, which is why Tiberinus used her in the first place – only a special kind of witch could have survived being used like that in the HBG."

"She has rejuvenating powers!" Korinna blurted.

"Yes. And now she's linked to Dawn's magic, her blood must carry something even more special – an ability to conjure a kind of rebirth."

"Like she could reset Trip to what he was before!"

"Yes."

"Goddess. That's amazing. It's like what the old Gods used to do when they needed to share power or heal or just power-up. They'd even grow fangs to help facilitate it."

"Like Tiberinus did to Ilia," Tamuel said harshly.

Korinna's eyes flared wide. "Oh no."

"What?" Trip asked as Korinna began to wring her hands.

"If she knows this, she'll never come."

"What?" Trip's gaze zipped from one to the other. "Why?"

Tamuel grimaced. "It's the blood thing."

"The blood?"

Korinna grimaced. "Well, that's a rather long story about lies and betrayal, leading to her being held prisoner in a gem for thousands of years. Suffice it to say, she won't be on board with any kind of blood magic. Especially if you have to drink it."

He pointed at the ring and the blood that still stained its surface. "Do you hide your use of it from her?"

"No. It makes her uncomfortable, but she knows it's got more to do with the magical qualities in my blood tied to my birthright, and so isn't like the blood magic she fears. However, drinking blood to syphon power, even if it's to heal ... I don't think we'll be able to talk her around to accepting that as anything but evil given her past."

No. This couldn't be true. "But she's been coming to me. She told me."

"It wasn't her."

"It was. She remembers the dreams. She's seen them too. I know she has, otherwise you wouldn't be here."

"That's true," Tamuel said. "But I know Ilia. I lived with her and the gem in my chest for months. She would never ask you to drink her blood. You said it didn't sound like her voice when she asked you to do that, right?" Trip nodded. "Something else is at play here, putting those words in her mouth."

"The same thing that brought her the book?"

"Perhaps," Tamuel said, expression becoming even more grim.

Damn all the devils in all the Hells! He was so close. For the first time in his very long existence, he knew he was close to remembering what he was supposed to be; who he was. But if Korinna and Tamuel were to be believed, being close wasn't going to get them anything. He would continue to live his life not knowing what all this was for. He would never know why this woman who stood in front of him was suddenly so terribly important to him. He would never know why his blood grew things and he never aged. He would always be alone.

Even though he'd always thought that was his future and was resolved to it, the possibility that had been waved in front of his face for a brief moment, of something more, of true, long-lasting connection, now made that future unbearable.

Despair took him in its maw.

Why was his life like this? Who had done this to him? There were no answers and there were never going to be any.

He turned to stare across his lands.

As he did, Ilia appeared on the other side of the field. She didn't look like she had previously – this time far more ghost-like. In fact, he could see the outline of the land and trees behind her. She smiled at him, blew him a kiss then turned and walked through the fence and up the hill, disappearing among next year's crop of pine trees.

"She's here."

"Who?"

"Ilia. There she is. Rising above the trees. Oh. She looks like a Christmas angel."

"I can't see her."

They couldn't see her? But suddenly it didn't matter as her voice, deeper and huskier than he remembered, sounded in his ears.

"Look at these pine trees you grow. They could be nothing, withering and dying without the right care. But, you give them everything they need so they can become healthy and green and stand as a sign of the promise of renewal. Hope is like that."

"It is?"

"Yes. It's like these trees, you can make hope grow and flourish once more. You love this time of year for a reason — because it speaks to the need in your soul for family, love and forgiveness. Remember that now and go forth, in the spirit of Christmas, and find a way. Find a way to me. Find a way for me. I need you." She gestured behind him. *"Your daughter needs you. Find a way."*

"What?"

"You know."

"I do? How?"

"Who are you talking to, Trip?"

Before he could answer Korinna's confused question, Ilia disappeared in a flare of light as bright as the star of Bethlehem.

"What the fuck was that?" Tamuel said, shielding his eyes.

"Trip? Trip, are you okay?"

"Did you see her?" he asked, still unable to look away from where she'd hovered moments before.

"See who?"

"The morning star. The dawn's light. My Christmas angel. Ilia."

"What? No. She couldn't be here. She can't leave without Dawn."

"All I saw was a bright flare of light."

He shook his head. It didn't matter that they hadn't seen her. All that mattered was that he had. "She was here and she gave me a message." One meant just for him because only he could figure it out. Only he could bring it to pass. Because only he had lived the life that he had leading up to this very moment in time.

The trees. His Christmas spirit. His love of what this time of year represented: light and laughter and sharing, the warmth of family and friends, the renewal brought around by kindness and forgiveness. They were true and everlasting, no matter if you believed in the old ways or the newer religions that had taken them as part of their celebrations.

The black of depression and despair faded. He spun to face Korinna and Tamuel. "I know what to do!"

Korinna blinked rapidly at his startling announcement. "Know what to do what?"

"To encourage her to agree. To see it's not evil. To make this work."

"You do?" Tamuel asked, putting his arm around Korinna. "How can we help?"

A smile curled his lips. "You can get her here, right? Ilia?"

They both nodded, Tamuel asking, "But what good will that do?"

"And you will stay?"

"Of course." Korinna said, taking his outstretched hands. He sighed happily at the feeling of oneness and homecoming that holding her hands brought to him. By the smile in her eyes, he guessed she felt the same way.

"Good. Then, invite Ilia and everyone who needs to come with her. We will share Christmas together and see if it won't shed a little of its Christmas magic and help us out in the way we need it to."

"You're hoping for a true Christmas miracle then," she said, not a little sarcasm in her tone.

He didn't care if she doubted. She would learn. "Not hoping. I am certain we can make one happen." He slung an arm around Korinna, the other around Tamuel and, guiding them towards his ute, said, "Now, tell me what you can."

"But what about the pain?"

"If I pass out from it, we'll know not to touch on that until I get my memories back." He squeezed Korinna's shoulder, grinning like a loon. "Now, we better get to it. There's a lot to do to get everything ready before they arrive."

As they got into the ute and drove back to his house, he could barely contain his excitement.

Soon, very soon, he would remember everything – the good and the bad.

He couldn't wait!

THIRTEEN

She was coming. Today. In fact, she'd be here with Tamuel's family later this morning.

It was like a buzz under his skin, the knowledge, the certainty. He'd known it this morning before he'd even seen Korinna, who'd greeted him with the news.

She was so close now. And with her came the future. His future.

Or was it his past?

One was all tangled up in the other – for without a past, how could you have a true future?

For the first time in his life, he wished he didn't have hundreds of Christmas tree hunters coming today. He wished he had the day free, set aside just for her. For her arrival. For the momentous *something* he knew she brought with her.

He glanced around. The car park was almost full. Daphne and Charlie were already in their summer-friendly Mrs Claus and elf costumes and were busy confirming the e-tickets for each booking.

There was a queue lined up around the shop-shed,

where Harry and Gideon were stationed along with Korinna, ready to greet hungry and thirsty travellers with a cold drink and whiskey cake before they headed off to hunt down and cut their trees. Tamuel was acting as traffic officer in the car park – also in an elf costume.

The nine o'clock session of Christmas tree hunters was about to begin. He couldn't ask them to go now and disappoint all these people. Part of his plan was about the Christmas spirit, about spreading and sharing the joy. Their being here was part of who he was and why he did what he did. He needed Ilia to see that. To feel it. To understand what sharing herself in the way he needed her to would do for them; for the world.

But not only that, deep in his bones, he knew that once he drank of her blood, things would be righted for them in a way they never had before.

He had to show her, to make her see. And this was the only way he knew how.

Daphne glanced his way, her brow rising in question. He waved and smiled in acknowledgement, then headed to get changed into his costume, nerves fluttering in his stomach.

She and the boys had been worried at first that Korinna and Tamuel were lying. That they were some kind of gold-digging couple come to benefit from his prosperity. But nobody who looked at him and Korinna could deny the familial connection.

Korinna had smoothed things over with the story that her mother, his high school sweetheart, had never told Trip she was pregnant because she didn't want to hold him back from his plans of travelling the world once they finished school – which cleverly explained how, at his age, he could have a daughter in her late twenties. Only after her mother's recent death had Korinna discovered his identity and tracked him down.

It helped too that both she and Tamuel were so kind and helpful – with wealth of their own given how they dressed and the helpful additions they'd made to the farm and its Christmas decorations. So it hadn't taken long before they had Daphne and her boys onside.

Daphne hadn't even baulked when she found out Trip had invited them and their family down for Christmas so they could all get to know each other at this most special time of year.

Daphne had immediately started planning menus for the next few weeks and things to do with their visitors once they got here. He was a little worried that he would have no time with Ilia as he tried to work some Christmas magic on her and get her to agree to the horrible reality that he must drink her blood, but both Korinna and Tamuel said they'd help with that.

There were so many unknowns though. Ultimately it came down to Ilia being willing to give while he only took, but there was nothing he could do about that other than focus on bringing the joy and family feeling that would convince her that drinking her blood was for good purposes, not evil.

He ducked around the back of the shed and slipped inside his workshop. He grabbed his Santa suit off the hanger and headed into the change-room. He was actually glad he had something to do now to while away the time before her arrival.

Fifteen minutes later, dressed the part and having made certain the tractors and their trailers were all ready to go – and laughing at the amount of tinsel-covered gaffa tape Harry and Gideon had used to stick the antlers and red reindeer noses on the tractors – he hopped on to the one closest to the door, started the engine and with a rumble, drove out of the garage.

"Ho, ho, ho. Merry Christmas!" he called out as he drove around the corner and up to where people waited, eating whiskey cakes and drinking frosted cups of fruity tea that Korinna was passing around. "My trusty steed Rudolfer and I are ready to go Christmas tree hunting. Who's ready for a ride on my Aussie sleigh to come and hunt with me?"

Shrieks of 'me' lit the air as hands were thrust up, most of the kids grasping a candy cane that they'd already been given from the sack Gideon hauled around.

Trip laughed jovially and said, "Once you've finished your drinks and cake, those with a one on their tickets, hop on in. Those with a two, my helper-elf, Charlie, will be out with the other sleigh in a moment to take you to where the best tree hunting will be this year. Climb aboard and a-hunting we will go!"

Gideon and Harry helped everyone up as the sound of the second tractor chugging out of the garage lit the air. Cheers went up as Charlie drove it around the corner towards those waiting for him.

As soon as both groups were loaded up, he set off, winding up the hill towards this year's crop of trees.

The laughter and happy chatter carried to him over the rumble of the tractor engines and made him smile. This was what he loved.

ILIA HAD RECOVERED QUICKLY after the incident with the book draining her and Dawn's souls to power her vision, but the baby had not. It had been agonising to see her so listless as

Bas and Violetta worked their magics and slowly brought her back to them. She'd tried syphoning some of her energies back through the link that tied them together and into the baby, but Bas and Jules had instantly noticed and demanded she stop.

"All you're doing is making yourself weaker, which isn't good for you or Dawn," Bas had said firmly. "Let Violetta and I take care of her."

"And for pity's sake," Violetta had said. "Don't touch any more books."

Not being able to do anything was frustrating, made worse by the fact Korinna and Tamuel were waiting on them all.

Their news had been the only light in a dark week. It was annoying that Trip couldn't come up to Melbourne, but given he ran a Christmas tree farm and this was December, she supposed it was difficult for him to leave. It wasn't like this was going to take a few minutes – there was much to discuss and the problem of returning his memory to overcome. So down to Tasmania she had to go. Which meant all of them had to go.

She'd been certain Jules and Bas would say no given Dawn's state and Jules' own plans for Christmas, but they'd readily agreed to the trip as soon as baby Dawn was recovered.

During the week while Dawn recovered, Triptolemus – or Trip, as Korinna had reported that he liked to be called – continued to feature in her dreams. Frustratingly, the dreams never went any further than they had. It was as if something was blocking them from taking that extra step and no matter how much she tried to push them to move forward, it never happened. She'd always woken in a sweat, panting and tingling all over with a need that just didn't want to be sated no matter how much she took things into her own hands.

It was a relief on the Saturday morning when they finally set off on their trip to Tasmania – a trip which soon became a horror from which there was no escape. Dawn had begun to cry and vomit the moment the plane took off and continued the spew-fest in the car they hired to drive to Trip's farm.

It seemed that travelling via portal wasn't the only kind of travel the baby didn't like – although this wasn't as bad as the portal travel had been. Still, she felt horrible for the poor little mite, but even worse was to discover that she was a sympathetic vomiter. Or a sympathetic dry-retcher. By some miracle she'd managed to keep her breakfast in her stomach where it belonged. She'd thank the Gods, but didn't want to give them credit for even that much.

And quite frankly, much more of dealing with the bile-laden scent of baby sick and her breakfast wouldn't remain where it was. If only she could crack open her window – but when she'd done that, Dawn had begun to scream, so she'd quickly closed it.

To have been locked in a gem for thousands of years then to be freed and made human once more only to deal with the ignominy of this! But really, who was she to complain? Poor little Dawn had suffered so much worse and none of it was her fault. She was as caught up in the machinations of the Gods as Ilia was. That fact made her so angry.

And with that anger came the glow.

Dawn began to scream and retch more.

Shit. Crap. Fuck.

Given the smell in the car, deep breathing exercises

were out. So she had to find another way to calm the fire of fury inside her.

Her mind immediately threw up an image of Trip. And not just any image. The one of him smiling at her in that way he had just after he'd said all those lovely things about her.

The flare of rage inside her flickered and died, replaced by a curl of something heated, much lower, and curiously, a strange warmth around her heart.

Thinking about him like this calmed her in a way the sexy dreams didn't. Why? She didn't know. Just another mystery surrounding him. She wished she knew what tied them together in this way. She'd been looking for him, but something deep inside told her that wasn't why she'd begun, and continued to, have the dreams of him and had then been pulled into those astral visions.

The uncertainty of it troubled her. She didn't believe in coincidences. No, this felt much more like the Fates or some God or Goddess messing with her once again.

And she didn't like it one bit. Even though, she had to admit, she rather liked Trip. Not just because he was hot and she'd seen him naked and, oh boy, she definitely wanted to explore his glorious body. But because he was kind and gentle and loved growing things and helping people. Which made him unlike any other God or demi-God that she'd ever met – except for Bas and Tam of course.

She had felt excited to finally see him in the flesh, but with this realisation of more God-like meddling, and a deeper connection that whispered of something more than a good romp in bed with a sexy man, she now felt like she was heading towards her doom.

A shiver rippled over her skin and down her back.

She must have made a sound because Bas asked, "Are you okay?"

She forced a smile that didn't feel at all convincing, so she gave up on it and said, "Fine. I just want to get there."

"You and me both." His gaze flew to his daughter then back to the road.

Ilia rubbed the shiver out of her arms and turned to smile encouragingly at her tiny friend. Dawn's teary eyes met hers and somehow, despite how travel sick she was, the baby managed to smile.

Ilia returned the smile before whipping back to face the front. "How much further?" she asked Bas.

His gaze flicked to the sat-nav. "About twenty minutes."

"That long? Why does Trip have to live in the middle of nowhere, Tasmania?"

"Patience is its own reward," Violetta intoned from the back seat as Jules began to sing another lullaby to Dawn to try to get her to sleep.

"Patience kept me locked in a gem for almost 3000 years, so excuse me for not being a fan of its rewards."

"Patience got you out of that gem in the end."

She snorted. "Reward indeed."

"I know you don't mean that," Bas said, his deep voice a rumble beside her.

She swallowed hard and looked down at her hands. She'd picked the quick of her thumbnail raw. "No, I don't. I'll be forever grateful to all of you for what you did to free me."

"We know," Jules said in a breath between lullaby lyrics.

An annoying burn started at the back of her eyes. She sniffed and rubbed at them. "Bloody hay fever!" she said when she noticed Bas giving her the concerned side-eye.

He huffed a laugh and said, "Yeah, that kind of 'hay fever' has been bad for all of us this last year."

She glowered at him.

He masterfully ignored her as he took a rather sharp turn, then pointed to a hill rising before them. "Ah, we must be close. That hill is covered in Christmas trees. And look, there's the sign."

Sure enough, a large sign in green and red, all sparkly in the sun announced: Snowy Hills Christmas Tree Farm – Come for a tree, stay for the Christmaspalooza!

Hells-bells and all its demons.

Bas chuckled and she turned to see him glance at her quickly before returning his attention to the road. "Cheer up. A bit of Christmas won't kill you."

How had he figured out how she felt?

He chuckled again and said softly, "All the running away from Jules' Christmas madness has been a bit obvious."

"Bah humbug!" she grumbled.

That made him chuckle again. "I'm sure it won't be that bad."

"Little do you know." She stared blindly out the window, crossing her arms over herself to cover the shiver that wracked her again. Her suspicious and grumpy attitude had served her well over the span of her lifetime after being trapped in the HBG, and she wasn't about to change her stripes now.

Bah humbug indeed. She would give Scrooge a run for his money and no ghosts of Christmas Past, Present or Future would change her mind about one skerrick of it.

~

HOURS PASSED HAPPILY and Trip was almost able to ignore the feeling of electricity building inside him. But when he pulled up in front of the shop with the last of the second group of the day, their Christmas trees in Charlie's trailer behind him, a prickling started over his back, making him sit bolt upright in his seat.

He swung around to search the car park.

There was nothing out of the ordinary – people were leaving with their trees netted up and strapped to the tops of their cars or poking out of SUV boots.

Except there – a car had just pulled in at a time when they were expecting nobody.

She was here.

A tall male with dark hair who bore a strong resemblance to Tamuel hopped out of the driver's seat. The front passenger door opened and sun glinted off hair filled with the colours of the dawn as *she* climbed out of the car.

His breath caught in his chest as she turned, her gaze finding him as quickly as his had found her.

She didn't move away from the car. In fact, she clung to the open door as if holding on for dear life. And the look on her face ... If the Hells had an expression, that would be it.

Even with that look of doom and horror on her face, her beauty and the immediacy of her presence hit him like a punch in the diaphragm.

He tried to breathe, but it was impossible.

The world swung in front of him, darkness encroaching on the edges of his vision, and then slowly and unceremoniously, he fell off the tractor in a dead faint.

CHAPTER

FOURTEEN

"Did that Santa just faint? Bas, perhaps you should go and help him," Jules said as she pulled Dawn out of her car seat.

"He probably just tripped. Or it's a play they put on or something. Isn't there some movie where Santa falls off the roof?"

"And dies," Jules said as she moved to stand beside Ilia. "The father who finds him ends up having to take over the job of Santa."

"Well, bags that's not me."

"Bas!"

"It's him," Ilia said, still clinging to the door.

"That was Triptolemus? Bas, go help him!"

Bas muttered a curse under his breath before taking off towards the fallen Santa.

"Ilia? Are you okay?"

No. She wasn't. Far from it. How could just laying eyes on Triptolemus affect her like this? Longing and need filled her with warmth and a trembling that had nothing to do with lust. To cover her weakness and confusion, she snapped, "You know, I'm sure he'll be fine. Idiot shouldn't be wearing such a stifling suit in this weather."

"She's right," Jules said. "It's probably heat prostration."

"I'll go help Bas," Violetta said. "It's not like we can help him with magic. Not with all these people around."

Jules nodded towards the commotion where Korinna and Tamuel were pushing their way through the gathered crowd, Bas close behind them. "You better remind them. By the looks of things, Korinna might just forget."

"I don't know what you're worried about," Ilia said to Jules as Violetta hurried off. "Triptolemus is a God or demi-God or whatever. He'll be fine!" She on the other hand felt like she was dying a little bit inside.

Overdramatic? Perhaps. But kind of true.

Everything was buzzing and fizzing and yet slowing down – fading, fogging.

"Ilia!"

Pain flared as she hit the dirt. Shouts sounded around her. Then arms went under her and she was lifted up, the movement making the world swirl around her.

Her eyes fluttered open to land on Tamuel, his elf hat and ears looking precariously tipsy on his head. "Nice costume," she muttered.

He glanced down. "Thank the Gods you're okay."

"Am I?" she asked before passing out.

Somewhere deep inside her mind, she was aware of being carried, worried whispers, the sound of a woman's voice she didn't recognise telling them to bring her and Trip inside and telling people named Charlie, Harry and Gideon to take care of things out there and reset for the afternoon. She had no idea why any of that was important.

But then the fuss faded and she lost all sense of herself

as the world turned grey and stars swirled around her in a sickening way.

Oh Gods! It was just like when she'd been sucked into the HeartsBlood Gem!

She couldn't remember a spell or blood magic being used but it was almost exactly like the experience of being ripped from her body as Tiberinus drank her blood, her soul sucked into the gem he pushed against her.

No-no-no-no-no-no! Not again! How could this happen to me again!

How? Why? What had she done to deserve this?

Nothing.

Not. One. Damned. Thing!

Rage filled her, huge and fiery, a tight ball in her chest that pulsed out and out and out as words formed in her mind to curse the being responsible for this. "I vow—"

"Whoa! Hold your roll, little missy!"

Hands grasped her shoulders abruptly, stopping her from spinning out of control in the grey and the sparks of light. She gasped at the suddenness, her rage still there, still a huge thing inside her, but kept at bay by the shock of being grabbed and spoken to like that. "Little missy! What are you? A cowboy?"

He laughed. "Some people think of me that way. I prefer to think of myself as a little bit of mischief."

A little bit of mischief? Who in the Hells was this? She tried to focus, but the light wasn't good. Everything was monochrome except for the pinky-orange glow coming from her chest. In that glow, all she could see was a male-shaped figure as he held her still while they floated in the greyness of this nothing place. "Who are you? What are you doing here?"

"I am here for you and Triptolemus."

"Okay." His voice was so familiar, but she couldn't place it. Even so, a little bit more of her anger drained away. "Is he okay?"

"He's just dandy."

She looked around her. "So where is he?" She really wanted to see him. Out of that stupid Santa suit.

"Waiting. We had to stop on our journey because you decided to go all nuclear on me."

"Wait, what?"

"You were powering up, your magics and were about to use them to explode the in-between. And I couldn't have that now, could I?"

"Couldn't you?"

"No. Also, you were about to make a rash vow – and the Lords of the Hells know, there's been far too many vows bandied about by you people over the years. I had a chance to stop one of you from making another stupid proclamation that would make my job so much more difficult, so I did."

"Okay, so all of that maybe explains the what-are-you-doing-here part of my question. But it doesn't answer the who-are-you part?"

"Ahh, well, I was hoping to keep that to a once-and-I'm-out kind of thing."

She shook her head, his round-about way of speaking giving her a sudden headache. Or maybe that was due to the fact she'd passed out and hit her head. "What are you talking about?"

"Let's go to Triptolemus and then I will tell you all." The shadow tipped his head. "Well, actually, that's a lie. I won't tell you all. Can't. But I will tell you what you need to know for now to get yourself out of this shit you're in. It would have been so much easier if you hadn't fought me like you have." He took her hand before she could respond to any of that and said, "Come."

Then they were flying again through the grey with its sparkling stars, but this time, there was no spinning, so she actually got to look around. Not that there was much to look at. Except, yes, there *was* something, in the distance. A pinprick at first, that looked like a strangely red star, but grew slowly until she realised it was some kind of portal.

She couldn't see through it – it was filled with a red-grey fog – but its edges spun and ruby and garnet sparks lit the space around them.

It was kind of beautiful.

But she didn't get long to appreciate it as they were suddenly flying through it.

To land in a field where a lone male stood.

He turned as they appeared through the portal, his eyes meeting hers.

Electricity. Fire. Sparks of all sorts. Plus that strange warm weakness she'd experienced when she'd seen him in that stupid Santa suit on that ridiculous tractor. They shot through her. Gods! She was more alive than she'd ever been in her life. She wanted nothing more than to reach for him, touch him, press up against him, the warmth of him against the warmth of her, and never let go.

It was insanity.

And yet, nothing had ever felt so true. So real. So complete.

And so fucking scary.

"What's going on?" she breathed.

Triptolemus shook his head. "I don't know. I saw you then everything went blank and then I was here." He pointed behind her. "He told me to stay and he'd be back soon."

She wanted to look at the male who'd brought her here, but couldn't take her eyes from Triptolemus. He was glorious. Still in that silly Santa suit, but without the hat and beard – he was holding those. But this Santa suit looked like no Santa suit she'd ever seen, the way he was wearing it now. The front was undone, showing not the pillowy cushioning that had broken his fall when he'd tumbled off the tractor, but the suntanned planes of his broad, muscled chest, his Santa pants hitched low on his hips, showing off that 'v' of muscle that led down to what she knew was his glorious manhood. They were like arrows pointing to a place of glory – one she wanted to see again. Maybe suck on like the most delicious lollypop before chucking off her clothes and shucking off any final inhibitions she might have to ride him like nobody had ever ridden a Santa before.

"Okay. Wow. You two really need to cool down or you're going to combust this place. And if you combust my little slice of the in-between, daddy's gonna be a little pissed."

The words broke through her sexual fantasy and she snapped back into her body with a little pop. By the look in Trip's eyes, he'd been having a similar fantasy. What the Hells? She couldn't seem to control herself whenever she saw him. It'd been getting worse since she'd first spoken to him in his field that day, taking over her life more and more. It was scary as fuck and yet, it felt so right. Like seeing him was coming home.

She shook her head, trying to sort herself out, but her thoughts were mostly a jumbled mess, tangled up in the ever-growing want and need for him. His gaze on hers. His hands reaching for her. That smile tilting his glorious lips. The warm pine and spring rain scent of him that twined around her. She longed for his touch, his heat, his hardness to surround her and fill her as those lips of his met hers and then took her on a journey around her naked body of glorious, building expectation as he joined with her and drove them both to their very own slice of heaven.

After which she wanted to hold and be held and never let go. Hells – the need for that was even greater than her need to ravage him and be ravaged by him.

"By the Gods! I didn't realise the Fates had bound your souls. If I had, I would never have bothered with the introductory dreams. But what's done is done and can't be undone."

Once again she was pulled from her fantasies by the male's annoyingly amused voice. But she still couldn't turn to face him, or seem to ask him what the fuck he was talking about and why he'd brought them here. All she could do was stare at Trip. At the breadth of skin exposed by his open Santa suit. Her fingers tingled, the need to touch, to spread her palm over his chest, all that muscle twitching as she stroked and stoked the fire that was ready to combust between them.

She sucked in a shuddering breath. Trip did the same. Her gaze flew to his.

In his eyes she saw the same bewilderment, the same questions, roiling around inside her. But she could also see that he too was slayed by this overwhelming *need*. Something in his eyes that filled up all the empty places and made her feel ... whole.

She took a stumbling step towards him, hand outstretched.

He did the same.

The male stepped between them. "I can see now I might have made a slight error in calculations, although why you two couldn't have sated this need in the dreams, I don't know. but seriously, you have to pull yourselves together if we're going to get anywhere with this."

Taking in a shuddering breath, she finally managed to look at him. Her eyes popped wide as she took in the tall, thin, well-muscled, black-haired male with eyes that swirled with black and red and green, hinting at an old, old, power. And an old, old madness.

"You!" She'd seen him earlier that year when she'd lived in Tamuel's chest. He'd helped them ... kind of ... because he was an old friend of Tam's.

"Moi?" the male said, hand to his chest, lips trembling with mirth. "Yes, I am me. Very clever of you."

"What? No, I mean, you're Loki!"

"Ah, ah, ah!" he said, wagging his finger side to side. "I am not Loki." Wind whipped up, his hair flying like wings away from his face as a red-gold glow surrounded him, his voice echoing and loud, like a voice-over from a movie trailer as he said, "I am the Ghost of Christmas Past."

"You are?" Trip asked as Ilia stood there, mouth open, eyes wide.

Loki sketched an absurdly elaborate bow, all hand flurries and bending down to almost touch his feet, before popping back up again. "At your service. As requested."

"What?" Ilia spat. "You requested this loon to pretend to be the Ghost of Christmas Past? Are you insane?"

Triptolemus frowned. "I don't think I did any such thing."

"Of course you did." Ghost of Christmas Past-slash-Loki grinned widely. "You asked the Gods for help with your little plan, did you not?"

"I ..." he began, frowning deeply. "I had a plan, but I didn't ask for this." He looked around at the green field they stood in, surrounded by a forest of ancient pine trees that stretched up to the improbably blue-blue sky.

"Well, of course you didn't, because you weren't thinking big enough. But not to worry. I heard your plea and voila!" A hand flourish, another snap of wind, and a ruby red cape appeared around Loki's shoulders as his hair turned white and a beard grew to obscure the dimple in his chin. "Dressed for the part and all! How good am I?"

"Loki! Stop your nonsense and tell us why you brought us here!" Ilia snapped, wondering why she'd found him so amusing at Easter.

Loki pouted, swirling his cape around him like a chastened child. "But don't you like my cape? I went all out with it. See, it even has 'Ghost of Christmas Past' bedazzled on the back." He swung around, holding the cape wide to show them. "Just in case you confused me with the other two."

"What other two?"

"The Ghosts of Christmas Present and Future. I've got costumes ready to go for them too. Can't wait for you to see them. They're pretty spectacular if I do say so myself."

"What the Hells are you talking about?" Ilia shouted. "This is not a joke!"

Loki's eyes widened with offence. "A joke? Oh, no. This is not a joke. This is very, very serious. Especially if you two don't get your shit together and do what must be done."

Ilia opened her mouth to do some more shouting, but Triptolemus got in first.

"What must be done?" he asked quickly, a lot less shouty than she thought Loki deserved.

Loki turned to him, eyes flashing red and green like the lights on a Christmas tree. "We must go back to the past to save the future!"

CHAPTER

FIFTEEN

Wind whipped up around them, the green place they'd been in turning into a tornado, like colour being swirled into paint.

The tornado cleared as quickly as it had started and Trip found himself standing in a snow-tipped pine forest, Ilia and Loki opposite him.

"Ta-da!" Loki said, swirling his cape as he spun around in a circle, snow flying up in little flurries around his leg.

Ilia wrapped her arms around herself, teeth chattering, breath a puff on the air as she glared at him. "What is so 'ta-da' about this, you insane little shit?"

Trip understood her annoyance but didn't think it was exactly wise to annoy or upset the God who had brought them here. He was about to say as much, but Loki just laughed, the sound ringing joyously around them.

"Ah, I love a bit of spunk in a woman. If you weren't tied down to this one," a nod at Trip, "I might just allow myself to fall in love." He fluttered his long eyelashes at her as, with another swirling gesture of his cape, clasped his hands to his chest. "You truly are magnificent, Ilia. I understand now why Tamuel was so keen on helping you last year. You're a lucky God, Trip," he said, waggling his eyebrows.

Trip didn't respond because his mind had got stuck on one word. "God?" he asked through a throat suddenly parched like he'd not drunk for a thousand years.

Loki's face went through a series of puzzled expressions, before landing on an 'ah'. "Oops. A bit too soon with the news, eh? Have to admit though, I thought Korinna or Tam would have clued you in."

"They've mentioned things, but never anything about being a God. I thought I was a witch or warlock or something, like my daughter."

"Oh, she's so much more than a witch – she has your blood, after all. And you are so much more than a God – although that's the closest description so we'll stick with that for expediency's sake."

"What do you mean I'm more than a God?"

Loki rolled his eyes. "Did you not just hear me say we didn't have time for that?" He sighed dramatically. "All right. We don't really know what you are because there's nothing else like you."

"What do you mean by that?" Ilia asked.

Loki waved at her to be silent – she glowered at him – and said to Trip, "You grew out of the power wielded by Demeter, Persephone and Gaia themselves."

Trip winced at the names, but Loki went on.

"The child of many and yet not truly of one. An immaculate conception. Or accidental conception is probably more apt. A bit too much of them trying things out, sprinkling their powers around at times that proved ... birth-worthy. And suddenly there you were, grown out of Gaia's soil in amongst Dem's and Seph's favourite garden. A bit of a surprise. One they quickly got over when they realised what you represented for them, and what you could do."

"Is that why there's a bit of confusion about him in the texts?"

There were texts about him? This was crazy.

"Yes … and no. Demeter let some think he is a God and others think he is a demi-God. But he is his own creation, so to speak. Which is why his power holds dangers that Demeter and Persephone and Gaia did their best to keep hidden."

"Is that why they took my memories?"

Loki waved his hands. "No. That happened centuries after. Not until you had the misfortune of falling in love and spawning a legacy of your own."

"Korinna?"

He nodded.

"Why was having her so dangerous?"

"You were already a danger to the pantheons and their reigns, like the Gods were to the Titans before them. But add children to that mix …" Loki sighed and shook his head sadly. "Not good. Especially given the prophecy."

"What prophecy?"

"Well, that's what we're here for. A little blast from the past." He waved his hand. A shimmering mirror appeared before them. In it, they saw two women sitting before a pool of water. One of them touched its surface, face bowed, a long tangle of white hair hanging around her face. The other woman waited at her side, hand on the white-haired woman's shoulder.

"Tell me what you see, Cassandra."

"The ancient one. A Titan of old. Perses the Unknown, father of Hecate. He did not get caught with the others and sent into Tartarus. He was sent into the Void and trapped in the Beyond. The Gods thought that was the end of him. But he is strong and wily. He found his way out of the Beyond and is now in the Void seeking a way out. And that way out comes closer with Triptolemus and his child."

Her voice changed, taking on an echoing, mystical strain as she said:

"Their blood is what can bind him; their blood is what can find him;
Their blood is what can free him; their blood is what imprisons him.
In all of the Realms from Heavens to Hells
Expanding out to control the Eternal Well
All will be lost to Perses' mad need, an endless maw devouring all power
If control of the blood magic isn't held by the One and his progeny in the final hour."

"Well, that's enough of that." Loki waved his hand and the vision shifted.

"Wait! Is there something about a prophecy to do with me?" Ilia asked.

"Probably was, but if you see everything, what's the fun in that?"

"Fun? This isn't fun. This is life and death!" Ilia looked very much like she was going to clock him. And a strange glow emanated from her chest.

"Ilia. He's here to help."

Her gaze snapped to Trip's, eyes ablaze. "Is he? Can we be so certain of that? He is the God of Mischief, after all. He can't help himself. I mean, why waste time bringing us together in dreams? Why not just tell us what we need to know if it's so important? He could have saved us months and months of searching and stress and despair. But no, because he's a God, he has to do things the difficult way. The way most likely to piss people off and obfuscate the truth."

"The truth! You can't handle the truth!" Loki said, doing an exact impersonation of Jack Nicholson in that army movie Charlie and Harry had made Trip watch half a dozen times over the years.

Obviously though his impersonation-joke was ill timed because Ilia's fury sparked in her eyes, the glow in her chest getting brighter.

She turned on Loki, demeanour menacing, flames burning in her eyes, heat coming off her in waves. "The truth! All I ever wanted was the truth. But all I've ever got from you bloody Gods and Goddesses is lies and betrayals and secrets. I don't think a single one of you is capable of being truthful."

Loki pouted. "That's not fair. I can be truthful. It's just often not fun."

"This. Isn't. Fun." She stepped towards him with every word.

"Maybe not for you. But for me ..."

Trip grabbed Ilia's hand before she could raise it to punch Loki a smacker right in his smiling mouth.

At his touch, the glow in her chest dimmed.

Loki laughed, clapping his hand. "Such drama. Such passion. It's no wonder I could never keep control of the dream-visions."

"What do you mean?" Trip asked. "If you weren't in control, who was?"

Eyes opening wide, he let his gaze run meaningfully from Trip to Ilia.

"Us?"

Loki shrugged. "One of you? Perhaps both? But all that sexy stuff was definitely all you. Although, why you couldn't seal the deal, I have no idea."

Ilia looked away and Trip cleared his throat. "Umm, well, okay. But then what was your role?"

"All I did was put you together in the dreams because Demeter needed my help."

"But why would she ask *you* to help?" Ilia asked. "You're not even of her pantheon."

"Precisely the point. She could not show her hand, and she couldn't ask anyone she trusted in her pantheon to do so either, because same result – it would make her effort to hide you pointless. But who would look at little ol' me? I'm always doing something mischievous and silly. The Gods are so used to it now, they barely even glance at what I'm up to as long as it doesn't affect them."

"I still don't understand why she'd ask *you*. Why she'd trust *you*."

He touched a hand to his heart, flicking his hair back. "My innate charm and trustworthiness, obviously."

"Loki!" Trip snapped before Ilia could. "Be serious."

And suddenly, he was.

The wind stopped blowing his hair back from his face, his eyes stopped spinning green and red, and the cloak ceased its heroesque billowing. "I've never been more serious than I am in my duty to Demeter. She helped me when no other God or Goddess would in a moment of darkest despair; an action I can never truly repay. But even if that wasn't the case, I would have given my help when she asked for it. I have felt Perses creeping back. The darker side of my magics quivers and wishes to prostrate itself to the power he could wield if he ever escaped. And I vowed long ago that I would never again prostrate myself at the foot of another God. So even if you do not believe that I would do everything I can to ensure Demeter's plans succeed, believe that I will put myself and my wellbeing front and centre. Perses *cannot* have me or my powers. And to ensure that never comes to pass, he cannot fully be allowed back into this world."

"Fully?" Ilia asked. "That thing that came out of the Void at Easter – was that him?"

Loki nodded. "A small part of him. Call it a scout."

"It's scouting us? Then why have we seen nothing of it?"

Loki pulled a face. "Why do you think I'd know what's in the mind of a mad Old One? I have no idea what that scout is scouting, or even how it might report back. All I know is it's here and that, sooner or later, it will make itself known. It won't be able to stop itself. And when it does, you all have to be ready."

Trip stared at the other God, noticing out of the corner of his eye that Ilia looked worried, the glow in her chest now completely gone. "Then why play with us like you have? Why not just come out and tell us what we need to know if things are so dire?"

"Because while I have more freedom to act than Demeter does, there are still eyes on the lookout all the time. Rules that are in place regarding how information about certain forbidden subjects can and cannot be shared without drawing the ire of the greater Gods. I may be mischievous, but I am not foolish."

He crossed his arms, pouting a little. "Besides, I am not entirely to blame here. It's you two who couldn't seem to keep it in your pants. Every time I thought you were headed towards where you needed to go, you just kept dragging the visions right back to sexy-land. I should have realised then that you are soul-bound—"

"Soul-bound? What are you talking about?" Ilia said, jerking back a little. "We're not soul-bound."

"Of course you are. What do you think all of this ..." he waved his hand between them, "is caused by? This isn't just simple lust. You are meant to be."

Ilia paled, as if she was scared. But why? The thought they were meant to be together thrilled through him, making him happier than he'd ever felt in his life.

But he didn't have a chance to question her, because Loki tipped his head to the side and said, "Huh, that's probably why your blood more than any other is the key."

"My blood?" Ilia asked, paling further, fear now definitely clouding her eyes.

Trip tensed. Hells. It wasn't time yet for that to be brought up. She wasn't ready to know.

Loki waved his hand again, blithely ignoring her. "Of course, I can't be held to blame for missing such a thing. I mean, it's not like it happens that often. And I was just a little too frustrated by the fact my little plan wasn't coming together quite how I wanted. I have to say, it's been quite tiring constantly pulling you back into the dream-vision so we could attempt to get to the good stuff. I swear, it wouldn't have even happened if I hadn't done a little spell on that book and made it cough up the address when Trip failed to tell you in time."

"That book? That was you? That almost killed Dawn and me!"

"Uh-uh-uh, no skipping to the Ghost of Christmas Present act. We're still in the past. Now, on with the play!"

He waved his hand and another mirror appeared before them, wavering like before but quickly resolving to show the same tall woman, her green eyes shining with tears, standing before a man dressed in a Grecian-style tunic, shaking her head as he pleaded with her.

"This is when you came up with the plan," he said to Trip.

The scene sped forward to show them standing in this very forest, snow covering everything.

"This is where the spell was placed and you sacrificed everything for the good of us all." He raised a brow at Trip. "So honourable. Ah, but wait, this is my favourite bit." Demeter waved her hands and the ancient Trip stiffened, his face a rictus of pain, before he fell, to be caught and lowered lovingly onto the snow. A handkerchief appeared suddenly in Loki's hand and he dabbed at his eye and said wetly, "So touching. Brings a tear to my eye every time."

"Oh for fuck's sake!" Ilia grumbled.

"Harsh!" Loki said. "But hush. This bit is what affects you."

They watched as Demeter made her vow, hearing her words clearly and the three rolling knocks that followed, signifying the vow was accepted by the Eternal Well – unbreakable, unshakable, causing death if not brought to fruition.

"Why would she do that?" Ilia asked. "It wasn't even specific. How did she know she could do it?"

"She didn't. She just knew it must be done so made a vow to ensure it, no matter the cost." He turned his gaze to her, something in his eyes that was pointed and knowing, but that she couldn't understand.

"But ... I don't understand what this has to do with me? How am I a part of this?"

"Shortly after, she had a knowing about the gem and the spirit residing in it that she'd come into possession of. It was then she realised that you were the key to her completing the vow. It's funny how the Fates work, isn't it? Placing you in that gem so that you could then be of use when needed. An act of superior weaving, I have to say." He waved at the image again. "But look! This is where my Machiavellian mind truly came into its own for Demeter's plans."

They watched as the image played out, showing him bowed over the gem, Demeter behind him, a worried expression on her face. "You had already started to be able to make yourself known and she was worried you would use your persuasion on some poor bleeding heart to get you out."

"But nobody could get me out but Korinna and Tamuel. It was prophesied."

"I know. I was the one who came up with that prophecy," he said proudly, as if expecting congratulations. "Demeter was so grateful when I suggested it, because it was the only way to ensure you couldn't get free until in Korinna and Tamuel's hands. What she saw in her knowing was that you would only get to this point if they were the ones to free you."

Ilia stared at him, breath heaving. "You. Kept. Me. Enslaved. In. That. Gem. For. Three. Thousand. Years!"

"Uh-huh," Loki said, staring at the image of Demeter thanking him. "Pretty clever, huh?"

Ilia roared, lunging at him, the glow, like dawn's light, spreading in her chest once again, brighter this time.

Trip caught her as Loki went stumbling back, hands up. She screamed and fought against the arms banding around her. "Let me go! I have to kill him!"

The power in her chest didn't lessen this time at his

touch and was hot to the point of burning. But he held on. "No, Ilia. You can't. We need him."

"I don't need him. I don't need anyone."

"Ilia, please. Look at what's happening now."

Something in his voice made the fury hazing her sight and her mind fade just enough that she looked where he was pointing.

In the mirror a new image showed; one that was clearly of the present.

She and Trip lay on a bed, side by side, a glow surrounding them, their hands clasped.

Beyond them, Jules stood, sobbing, a limp Dawn in her arms. Bas, Korinna, Tamuel and Violetta gathered around her, hands raised above the baby, working their collective magics on her. But no matter what they did, she remained limp, face as pale as death, lips turning slowly blue.

"Dawn!" Ilia cried, the glow and her anger fading as quickly as they'd come.

"Ah, now we've got to the present," Loki said, spinning around.

His hair changed back to his normal black as his cloak turned into a black-hooded one covered in black sequins, except for the green ones on the back that spelled out Ghost of Christmas Present.

SIXTEEN

Ilia lunged towards the mirror. Trip let go of her just enough so she didn't face-plant into it. She would have thanked him except all her attention was on the precious baby in the image. "What's wrong with her?"

"She's dying."

Loki's tone was so cheerful it took her a moment to take it in. "She's dying?"

"That's what I said, isn't it?" He looked towards Trip as if seeking assurance.

Trip opened his mouth to say something but Ilia got in first. "What do you mean 'she's dying'? Why?"

"Because you're dying," he said pragmatically, waving his hand at her.

She blinked at him for a moment before words came to her. "What? No, I'm not." She pointed at her image. Both hers and Trip's bodies looked relatively healthy given their unconscious state.

"Ah, but you are." Loki wagged his finger, swaying a little so that his cloak fluttered around him. "You have been since you were made corporeal by Tamuel and that rather powerful little baby. A single life-force, no matter that it's as strong as hers, isn't enough to keep the both of you going."

"But ... there was no sign of this before."

"Ah, well, yes ..." Loki shuffled away from her again. "I'm afraid I might have just precipitated that a little – only out of necessity, of course."

"You what?"

"The dark magic book that I put in your way to help facilitate an astral visit with Triptolemus here ... It might have just sped things up a bit."

"How much is a bit?" Trip asked dangerously.

Loki shrugged. "Hard to know, really. You might have had a human lifespan to figure out how to separate yourself before. Now ... given how quickly little Dawny is deteriorating ..." Loki tipped his hand back and forth. "Probably Christmas day. Maybe a day less or a day more."

"What?" Ilia said, terror spiking through her as her gaze went back to the baby she'd give her life for. "This can't be. I can't let this happen. Tell me how to stop it from happening."

"Let Triptolemus drink your blood."

Once again, he said it so pragmatically that it took a moment before his words speared through her, but when they did, it was enough to pull her horrified gaze away from the mirror. "What?"

"You. Need. To. Let. Triptolemus. Drink. Your. Blood," he said slowly as if talking to someone who couldn't hear properly. And maybe she couldn't because she didn't want to hear what he'd just said, and yet she had.

Blood magic. He was suggesting blood magic! And not

just any type of blood magic, but exactly what Tiberinus had used on her.

Fear, huge and clawing, scraped at her insides, making it difficult to think, to breathe. She shoved it down, shoved it back. "You can't be serious," she said, voice shaking.

"I am very serious. What do you think all of this is about?"

"Umm, getting Triptolemus' memory back?"

"Which this will do."

She shook her head, trying desperately to hold onto reason, to not let the fear take her over. "B-but h-how does that help Dawn? I-I can't even s-see how it will help T-trip's memories c-come back."

"Well, I don't have time to get into the minutiae, but basically it comes down to the fact that the power you were born with, added to the power you got when you were reborn, not to mention the fact you are soul-bonded to him, makes your blood the ultimate cure-all for Trip here."

"But ... my original power wasn't anything special."

"The power you were born with is more than you ever thought it was. It is *very* special."

"Well ... I ... " She looked over at Trip but he seemed as lost in all this as she felt. "Even if that were true, I-I don't have it anymore."

"Of course you do. What do you think that hot little glow is that keeps leaking out of your chest?"

She stared at him, shaking her head, unable and unwilling to accept what he was saying. "B-blood magic isn't the answer here."

"Of course it is. It is the only answer."

"It's never an answer!" Ilia snapped, fist pressed against her chest as she struggled to breathe. The glow in her chest pulsed in response. She thought it only activated with anger, but it seemed fear flipped the switch on it too. She tried to shove it all down as she whispered, "Blood magic only brings pain and betrayal and death."

"But if it will help the baby ..." Trip said.

"You only want this because it will help you!" she snarled, turning on him. She'd been right to hold herself back from him. He was just like any other God – always wanting something from her. Wanting to use her and betray her.

He took a step back from her anger, but to his credit, kept his calm. "I won't lie. Of course I want that. But if you hadn't agreed, I would never have pushed the matter. I would have spent my life by your side trying to find another way. But this ..." He gestured at the image hanging before them. "That poor little baby. We have to do everything in our power to save her. Surely you want that?"

"Of course I do." Just the thought of Dawn's life in danger ... Her anger fizzled once again.

Trip wasn't to blame for this. No. The brutality behind all this had a touch of the Fates about it. No wonder she'd found that entry in the grimoire that said blood magic, under the right conditions, would sever the link between her and Dawn and had found nothing else to help her.

Well, she hadn't trusted the answer then and she certainly didn't trust it now. Breath unsteady, she said, "But ... This can't be the only option. Blood magic is dark magic. It trapped me and used me and has been the cause of so much misery in my life and in others. I mean, look at what it's done to you, Trip."

He frowned. "What do you mean?"

She began to pace, the words tumbling out of her. "This

is all happening because of the curse of blood magic. Perses means to use your special blood to break his way back into this reality, if what Loki has shown us is true. He means to use it for evil because that's what blood magic can only ever be used for."

"That's not true," Trip said. "Think what I can do with my blood. I grow things. I take something that is hardly living and make it flourish, turning it into something vibrant and new."

"That's not blood magic. That's just something special in your blood because of how you were created." Which was why she could feel the goodness in his soul, the kindness that made him want to give and share joy.

Her thought of moments before was unfair. He was nothing like the Gods and Fates responsible for all this. She should have known that. After all, part of his legend was about him travelling the globe, sharing his skills and teaching humans how to provide for themselves. He stopped them from relying so heavily on the mercy of the Gods – which was always a good thing. Then he'd given up his beloved wife and unborn daughter to protect not only them, but everyone, from an evil none of them was strong enough to face at that point.

Even after losing his memory, he had still travelled, sharing his skills and good fortune where he could, even spreading the joy of this ridiculous time of the year with his Christmas trees and food and drink and endless cheer.

But even with all his goodness, his kind intentions, he didn't understand the true evil of blood magic.

He came to stand in front of her, stopping her pacing, and took her hands. Looking deeply into her eyes, he said, "Blood magic isn't any more evil than what I do with my blood."

"But it is. It's very different. What you do brings life. Blood magic just brings misery and darkness."

He sighed. "Korinna told me you'd feel this way."

"She did?"

He nodded. "In the last week, she and Tamuel have filled me in on so much. Including what you've been through." He let go of one of her hands and touched her cheek.

She couldn't help but lean into the gentle caress as she gazed into his beautiful eyes with their crystal green depths and long dark lashes.

"I'm so sorry for all that was done to you. For all that you've lost. And I truly don't want to ever ask you to do something you're not comfortable with." He snorted a self-derisive laugh. "It seems stupid now that I thought I could somehow win you around to allowing me to drink of your blood by showing you some Christmas spirit. I thought the joy or family bonds or something might be enough to convince you. But I didn't know. I didn't understand, until what Loki said, how you were kept trapped and used. And I'm so sorry for it."

"You are?"

"Of course. That only happened to you because of me. Because you are the answer to my current problem. We might not be responsible for what Tiberinus did originally, but there is no denying that the Fates ensured you could be here, ready once again to be used. This time, by me." He let out a shuddery breath, the expression on his face filled with so much regret, shame and pain. "And I wish right now that I could just set you free of it all. I wish that I could say it's not necessary, that you don't have to do this. I want to be able to do that. You deserve to be free. But ..." His gaze returned to the image.

At his sucked-in breath, she turned to see that things had become worse with Dawn.

It was now dark, the glow surrounding the two bodies on the bed lighting the room, showing clearly the little body lying limply beside them, her parents kneeling beside the bed, hands grasping their daughter's, Korinna, Tamuel and Violetta standing behind them.

"How much time has passed?"

"A week since you fell unconscious," Loki said.

"A week! But you said she only has until Christmas."

"I did say that, didn't I. Which means, if we take much longer here, it could be too late. See, even as we stand here, time passes and things become more dire."

The image shifted to show all the adults in the room next to the bed, hands out, pumping power and their own life-forces into the baby, trying desperately to keep her alive. But they were weakening. Two demi-Gods, a demi-God-witch, a normal witch and a witch with Goddess-given powers did not have the life-force energy to keep them going indefinitely. Only a God or Goddess, with their full connection to the Eternal Well, the well-spring of all Godly powers and life-energy, could do that.

But they were trying. They wouldn't stop trying. They would all give their lives for Dawn.

As would she.

She glanced at Loki and Trip. Both looked so grim, so ... grief-stricken. They didn't want to bind her or use her for evil or their own selfish machinations, but still ... How could she trust they all wouldn't end up paying some even worse price? Although, right now, she couldn't think of a worse price than losing Dawn.

As they watched, Violetta passed out, falling to the

floor, having given too much of herself to keep going. Hells. Was she dead? Had she already made that sacrifice?

"Loki. Stop this!" she pleaded, gripping his shirt, shaking. "Please. Make it stop."

"There's only one way. You must allow Triptolemus to drink your blood. When he does, the link between you should prove stronger than the one between you and Dawn, severing the current one in favour of a new one, and the baby will be free."

"She will survive?" She yanked at his shirt.

He frowned down at the hands crumpling his costume. "And so will you. And Trip will have all his memories back."

"But she will be tied to me?" Trip asked.

"Of course. You will be sharing your life-force with her. You will be the one keeping her alive."

"So, you're asking me to leash her to me? How is that any different from what was done to her when she was used to power that gem?"

"Because you are soulmates," he said, as if that was obvious. "You are already tied together by the Fates and destiny and the Eternal Well in a way that cannot be undone by any other. But if it truly bothers you, I'm sure you can keep looking for a way to free her life-force from yours in the years ahead. That is, of course, if we manage to defeat Perses. Which, if you remember, is the point of all of this."

"That baby should never have been endangered to get us to here."

Loki winced. "I have to admit, that was never a part of my plan. But it's not easy to wrangle the threads of fate into submission. You try it sometime."

"Don't you even care she's dying?" Ilia asked.

"Of course I care. That's why I brought you here, to

bring it to your attention and make you see what must be done. Because if I'm sure of anything, Trip's silly plan wouldn't have worked."

"What do you mean?"

"Let me show you some possible futures. Maybe then you'll decide."

CHAPTER

SEVENTEEN

Loki waved his hand over the image. It changed to show what was obviously Christmas day, given the wrapping paper strewn around the base of the tree and the half-eaten meal on the table beside it. But nobody was at the table, they were all standing around it, an argument in full swing.

"Where are Daphne and the boys?" Trip asked.

"Who?" Loki asked.

"My friends. They work with me on the farm."

"Oh." Loki shrugged. "Dunno. Tam probably spelled them to stay away from all the magic going on. Good thing too, given what's about to happen in this version of the future."

As they watched, the argument got more and more out of hand. Ilia couldn't believe the look on her face – betrayal mixed with an anger so deep it burned.

And the glow! It was coming out of her chest, expanding, growing brighter and brighter as Trip argued his case, and Korinna and Tamuel – the people she'd thought of as friends; the two people in all the world who'd always backed her up; who'd never let her down – took his side. The fury that lived inside her, fuelled by a total and utter need for retribution and revenge that had carried her through the ages, grew in the image. But now it was fuelled by the betrayal playing out in this version of the future.

It grew and grew and then exploded out of her, felling them all in one, horrifying burst.

Ilia stared, unable to blink or breathe, as her power, the power she'd never thought was much of anything, had thought was lost when she was freed from the HeartsBlood Gem, killed everyone in the room.

Humans. Witches. Demi-Gods. Goddess-gifted witches who were as strong as Gods. Even Trip was gone. Wasn't he supposed to be unkillable?

By all the fires in all the Hells, she *was* a God killer. *The God Killer.*

That was her.

"Oh Gods. Dawn," Trip whispered.

Ilia's gaze searched the image until she found what brought that broken sound to Trip's voice.

Attached as she was to Ilia, Dawn had been spared death. But death would have been better. The burst of power had pulled nearly everything the baby was from her, making her skin crack and bleed through terrible burns while she slowly withered as her life, her soul, was sucked from her and into Ilia. Feeding Ilia.

And the most horrible part of it all was that Dawn was still conscious, feeling all of it. Screaming. Such terror, such pain!

"No. No. Do something!" Ilia cried.

"There's nothing to be done," Loki said. "This would have been the future if I hadn't brought you here." He made a humphing sound, his expression flat as the scene played out before them. "If you think this is bad, wait until you see what happens next." He shuddered.

In the image, as the dust settled from her firestorm, the future-Ilia stared around her, tears flowing down her face to drop and sizzle on the still-burning embers of Trip's house. Slowly, so slowly, she moved towards the blackened, bleeding husk that was little Dawn.

She carefully knelt down beside the baby. Then holding out her hands, gripped a hold of the gossamer thread that was the link between them, and tried with everything in her to give back what she'd taken.

Some of the blackened skin around where the link joined them over Dawn's chest began to turn red, then pink. It was working! But not fast enough. The baby's breath was a slow shudder, her screams now mere whimpers as Death laid its foul hand upon her.

She felt future-Ilia's pain and grief, the guilt and desperation, as if it was hers now. Felt the *need* to do more. But she could also feel that there wasn't much more inside her – so much had exploded out of her with the fury that had caused this. There was power all around her though – in the remnants of what was left of those who'd been her family – and yes, she knew now they were her family. She'd been so stupid to deny the truth of it before.

And with that truth, she fell into the vision; became future-Ilia.

She looked around, eyes bleary with unshed tears she couldn't let fall until she'd done something to fix this. But there were no answers in the devastation around her.

Until her gaze fell once again on the bodies of those she loved with everything in her.

Despite the fact they were dead, their spirits had not yet departed and their power still buzzed in their flesh.

Power that was no longer of help to them, but it could be of help to her.

Bile filled her mouth at what she was thinking, but she was all out of options. Something had to come from the violence and death she'd wrought with her uncontrolled power.

Heart breaking, she flung her hand out, using the links she had with every single one of them – links of love, of friendship, of family – and then pulled from them. She took and took until first one, then another and another, was sucked dry and turned to dust, everything they were now inside her.

But it wasn't enough.

The baby was still dying.

Sobbing, desperate, she flung out her hand again and created a link with the greatest power around her – Gaia. She was only able to do so because of the power she'd taken from Trip and Korinna. It allowed her to tap into something that was sacred, divine. And she took and took and took.

And as she did, everything died around her; the light was sucked from the world and into her to power her guilt-driven furious misery as she desperately tried to save Dawn.

The baby slowly turned from blackened char to healthy pink, but still, she didn't wake.

She had to wake. She had to. Ilia couldn't stand it if she lost another baby.

But as she held Dawn, the baby took her last breath and passed out of this world.

Ilia screamed to the Heavens, her fury so great now that time and space split open under its force. In that split was the pulsing grey of the Void, and the fullness of evil that waited there.

With a shriek of victory, something huge and black and terrifying spilled out, tendrils, like fingers, gripping the edges of the tear, pushing it wider, wider. Then as the sky rent in two, the evil oozed down to cover the land, sucking up all the souls she hadn't already managed to destroy.

Ilia screamed as the evil drank her soul.

And then she was standing once again in the place Loki had brought them to, watching the mirror-like surface fog once more, hiding the image she'd been sucked into.

Her cheeks were wet, her breath coming in great heaving gasps, Trip's arm around her shoulder, holding her up. She swiped at her eyes and managed to say, "That ... that can't be true! I'm not the one Perses can use to get out of the Void."

"If you let your power take over you and then you take every other bit of power from this world, then you are."

"But ... I wouldn't do that!"

"You would," Loki said sadly. He tapped her chest where the glow remained even now. "You almost let your fury get the better of you multiple times since I brought you on this journey. If Trip or I hadn't stopped you, it could have been disastrous."

"But ... I ... I don't have that kind of magic. I can't take power from others."

"Of course you can. Why do you think the ghosts ran from you when you used your power to repel them? Why do you think they kept away?"

"Because my repelling spell worked?"

"No, because the magic you were created with, the birth magic for lack of a better word, is being twisted by your bitterness and fury. It can give and create, but it can also take and tear apart. You didn't just repel the ghosts, you started to undo them, taking the essence of them into your-self. They ran from you to save themselves."

"I didn't mean—"

"Of course you didn't." He waved his hand at the image. "Just like you won't mean to do this either. But the fact is, if you don't come to terms with allowing Trip to drink your blood, then this is the future we face."

"But ... if I know this is what lies ahead, I can avoid it. I can just say no."

"You can. But then this happens."

He waved his hand, showing another image. This time, rather than allow her fury to build, she simply refused them and walked out. Time sped forward to show her friends battling the evil that was Perses as he exploded from the Void and used Trip's and Korinna's blood to power himself, destroying all before him.

"I wouldn't leave them to fight alone. I'd be there to help."

"Yes. But without your blood giving him his memory, and you and Dawn being dead because you didn't find another way to separate from her, they fail. Even if you and Dawn are still alive, you are both too weak to be of true help." Another image showed her refusing, but staying to fight – and die – by their side as Perses once again drained Trip and Korinna of their blood and destroyed everything.

Before she could protest that possibility, another image followed, and another and another, a rolling horror of futures where she said 'no' and all of her friends died; and Hells on earth was born because of it.

"But ... but ... this can't be all on me. I'm nothing. I'm unimportant," Ilia said weakly as fresh tears streamed down her face. Her mind was in turmoil, a pain in her chest so bad it made it hard to breathe.

"We are all unimportant ... until we aren't," Loki said.

"That isn't very helpful, Loki," Trip said, glaring at the other God.

"I'm sorry. I've used up my quota of helpfulness in getting you to here. The rest is up to you."

"But ..." She cast around for some argument, some alternative. However, the only question to ask was, "How do I know that the future will be any better if I allow Trip to drink my blood and tie my life-force to his?"

"Good question," Trip said. "Show her that future."

Loki raised his hands. "I can't. Because of the blood magic, that future is uncertain. The only certainty I can show you is this." He waved his hand.

Jules was placing Dawn on the bed beside where Ilia sat. She was sobbing and couldn't seem to let go of her daughter's hand, stop touching her head. Ilia leaned over and said something to her, then Bas added something else. A short conversation passed between Jules and Ilia, ending with Ilia smiling, tears in her eyes. Then Jules kissed Dawn on the forehead before rising to stand by her mate's side, supported by him, her family at her back.

The Ilia in the vision took a deep breath as she lay down, then turned to Trip, muttering something.

He nodded, cupped her face and whispered words that made her eyes widen, then before she could respond, he bit down on her neck and began to drink.

A desperate kind of hope filled all their faces alongside terrified grief as the link – suddenly visible – between Ilia and Dawn began to fade. The baby's lips became a little less blue, her skin a little less deathly pale.

Within a few minutes, the link was so thin and tight that when Dawn's eyes snapped open on a wail, her arms flailing, the movement was enough to snap the bond completely.

She was free.

Her mother and father grabbed her up, their cries of relief and joy obvious even though there was no sound.

Loki waved his hand again; the image disappeared.

"Wait! What happens next?"

"That I can't show you." Loki turned to face her, a look of triumph glowing in his eyes. "But as you can see, the only clear option to save Dawn is to allow the blood magic."

"But we don't even know if doing that will ultimately save everyone."

Loki frowned at her. "Never happy are you? What about the fact you just saw yourself saving Dawn? I thought that would be enough."

Ilia's lips trembled. He was right. It was wonderful. She didn't believe it before, but she couldn't argue with what she'd seen. She could free Dawn if she allowed Trip to drink her blood. Still, the very thought made her skin crawl and her mind scream – and caused the power to glow in her chest once more.

Lip trembling, she said, "I want to do this. I'm just ... I'm afraid the fear ..." She gripped at her chest, scrunching her t-shirt up in her hand, the glow getting brighter. "It burns inside me, wanting out. I'm afraid that I won't be able to stop it from doing just that the moment you begin to drink."

"It didn't, though," Trip said, gesturing to the now-blank mirror surface. "Loki showed you."

"He showed to a certain point. If only I could see more, it would help allay my fear that it might be worse."

"Worse than what I just showed you?"

She gestured futilely. "You don't understand. I need …
something. Please, give me something."

Trip turned to face her, taking her hands in his,
squeezing gently. "He can't. None of us can. We just need to
trust. Trust in each other. Trust in ourselves. Trust that,
whatever comes, we are family by choice if not all by blood,
and we will stand together, facing whatever comes. And if
your power starts to overwhelm you, then we will face that
too. Together." He shot Loki a look. "That's what I wanted
to show her in the weeks leading up to Christmas. The
reason I love Christmas so much." His gaze met hers again.
"It's the Christmas spirit. Not just kindness and generosity,
but the fact that if we let it in, love and friendship and
family binds us together and makes us strong. I wanted you
to see that you are not alone in this. That this is something
we all do, together. That it gives all of us something as we
give something of ourselves."

He lifted his hands to cup her cheeks, thumbs brushing
along her suddenly sensitised skin. "I might drink from
you," he said softly, breath brushing over her face, "but I
also will be giving you life-force energy. You might give of
your blood, but you also get the freedom you want for little
Dawn. And even though you will be tied to me, I will make
certain it is not a bond you are restricted by." He dropped
his hands to her shoulders. "We will go wherever and do
whatever you want. This is my promise to you."

"After you've defeated Perses, you mean," Loki said
dryly.

"Of course. But maybe before that too." He winked at
Ilia and she couldn't help but offer him a small smile in
return, glad, despite everything, that he was holding onto
her. She needed his touch, to feel him there, with her. It
made coming to this terrible decision not seem so … lonely.

"So," Loki said, waving his hand again to show the same image of the present they'd seen before. Dawn dying. Her family devastated and helpless. She and Trip lying unconscious on the bed, seemingly useless, but in truth, the only answer to stop Dawn from dying. "Have we resolved things? Has this little trip with the Ghosts of Christmas Past, Present and Future done the trick? Are you ready to address the problem at hand?" He turned to look at her, brows raised.

She chewed on her lip, hands worrying in front of her.

The problem at hand.

That's what she needed to concentrate on. Not some future she couldn't control.

This. This is what she could do. This is what her life had been leading to, whether she wanted it or not.

She'd been unable to save her sons, but this baby's life was in her hands and she could save her.

Surely she'd be able to rise above her fear and just let Trip do what he needed to do?

He was right. She might be giving a lot but she was also getting what she wanted in return. Okay, it wasn't full freedom. But it was never really about *her* freedom. She'd only ever wanted freedom for Dawn. That little girl shouldn't have ever had to suffer being bound to Ilia.

Trip ... well, he was an adult who could deal with the consequences of being bound to someone as bitter and broken as she was.

"Ilia." Trip ran his hands down her arms to take hers in his once more, raising them to hold against his chest. His skin was so warm, his heartbeat a steady, sturdy drum-roll beneath her palms. "If you don't trust me, then trust yourself. Trust in the goodness I know you have inside."

"Goodness?"

He nodded. "Goodness. Look what you did, what you would sacrifice for love of that baby. You are filled with goodness, if you would only see it."

"I wish I could see me as you see me," she whispered.

A smile broke out on his face as he touched beside her mouth. "You will. You will come to see everything I see when you agree to this. You can't help but see it when your blood, powered by that goodness as it enters me, does everything we know it can, and more, as we fight for all that's good."

"How can you be certain?"

"That you are filled with goodness? You are standing before me, listening seriously to a proposition that terrifies you, all to save a baby and give my memories and my life back to me. What is goodness if not that?"

She huffed out a chuckle at his oversimplification and the fact he'd purposefully misread her question. "No. I mean, how can you be certain that it will all turn out right?"

He chewed on his lip for a moment. "I can't. But what's the alternative? A thousand futures filled with loss and destruction? Or a moment of faith that could lead to victory? Those are the choices before you. I hope you will choose faith. I hope you will choose to believe in me. But mostly, I hope you will choose to believe in yourself."

The warmth that radiated out from his touch was astonishing, making her catch her breath as it buzzed through her, filling her with something ... something ... wanted. Needed. And so big. But it was nothing as compared to his words. They filled her with something she hadn't felt in many thousands of years.

Filling her gaze with everything she felt inside, she said, "I believe."

His smile, it lit her up inside, as bright as the sun, calming the fury, dousing its flames. Then, still smiling at her, he said, "Right, Loki. How do we do this?"

"You wake up." Loki waved his hand and space wavered around them, swirling and dissolving; the only thing certain was Trip's grip on her hands, holding tight.

Then just before blackness took over and everything went away, she heard Loki say, "Damn it! I forgot to change cloaks. I'm still wearing the Ghost of Christmas Present. Odin be damned! What a waste of sequins!"

CHAPTER

EIGHTEEN

It was dark when Trip awoke in his bed. The room was quiet around him.

What time was it? For that matter, how did he get here? He couldn't remember coming to bed.

Hells. His head hurt.

He groaned.

Another groan sounded beside him. He flipped to his side to see Ilia.

She was awake and holding her head.

He didn't blame her. His felt rather like a sledgehammer had taken up residency and was busy marking every second with a thump against the inside of his skull.

But what was she doing there? How had she ...

It all came rushing back and he slammed upright.

"Oh-oh-oh. Don't move the bed like that. I'm going to chuck." Then, so saying, Ilia rolled over and vomited all over the floor.

Sympathetic vomiter that he was, he rolled over to the other side just in time.

The door opened, letting in a shaft of light from the

lounge room that slashed into his eyes. The thumping pain in his head blazed anew. "Yea Gods! Shut the door. Or turn the light off."

"They're awake," Tamuel shouted back into the lounge room.

There was a snort then a clatter as Korinna leaped up from the chair in the corner – she must have been sleeping – and rushed forward. Tamuel caught her before she could go more than a few steps. "Watch your step. They've both vomited."

"Let me take care of that," Violetta said, appearing behind them. She waved her hand and the smell of sick evaporated, replaced by a fresh citrus scent that helped clear the air but did nothing for Trip's nausea. He bent over and vomited some more. As did Ilia.

"Bas! We need you."

Tamuel's words echoed in Trip's head, adding to the pain of the sledgehammer. He held up his hand, managing to groan, "Please. Less noise. Less light."

Tamuel waved his hand and the light became a dull yellow glow.

Bas entered the room, his face shadowed with worry and fatigue. "Glad to see you're awake."

"Help her first," Trip said, pointing at Ilia as he pulled himself up gingerly to sit against the headboard.

Bas drew near the bed on Ilia's side, raising his hands, but Ilia grabbed his arm. "Where's Dawn?" she rasped.

His lips tightened, his breath hitching. "With Jules. Out there."

"She's sick?"

He nodded. "I can't seem to make her wake up. None of us can."

"Bring her in here."

"We just took her out there."

She shook her head slowly. "She needs to be here. It has to be exactly the same as what we saw or it might not work."

"What might not work?" Korinna asked.

"Healing Dawn. Making this all better."

Bas' eyes widened. "You can help her?"

Ilia's face contorted before she pulled herself together, and nodded. "We can."

"But how? How do you know?"

"Loki showed us."

"Loki?" Tamuel asked as he came to stand at the foot of the bed with Korinna. "What has he got to do with any of this?"

"No time to explain," Trip said, worry for the baby making him able to shove the nausea away and ignore the pain. "Dawn will die if we don't do something soon."

"But how?" Violetta.

"Why?" Tam.

"Because ..." Ilia sucked in a shaky breath, head dipping to stare at the hands she wrung in her lap. "I'm sucking the life out of her."

"What?" Bas snapped, taking a step back. "Why would you do that?"

"She can't help it!" Trip said, wanting to reach out to pull her to him, to comfort her, but any movement still made his stomach heave. So he simply said, "It's that damned bond Dawn created when she helped Tam make Ilia corporeal. Dawn is feeding her life-force."

"What?"

"How?"

"Why have we never seen this?"

The questions came from all quarters, pushing at him,

at Ilia, making her wince and curl in on herself a little more. Not a physical thing – she showed her strength in that moment by pushing herself upright with trembling arms – but a soul-thing he felt deep inside.

He wished he could stand between Ilia and Bas as the ex-cupid glowered at his love.

Yes, his love. He loved her. It had always been there, he realised now, but he hadn't truly known it until the moment she had taken that step of faith – for him, for the baby, for all of them – despite what it was doing to her. He loved her as he'd never loved before. Not even Korinna's mother, who he was as yet to remember. But he knew without needing that memory.

Loki was right. She was his soulmate, and he would die to protect her. He would die to protect her right to choose. To be her own person.

Except, because of a twist the cruel Fates had wound into his lifeline, he couldn't do any of that.

All he could do was stand strong beside her as she saved them all.

Then he would spend his life paying her back for everything she'd lost because of this Gods-cursed destiny that seemed to be their lot.

He would vow it, but enough rash vows had been made that took no prisoners in their need to be brought to fruition. He wouldn't add to Ilia's burden; not for anything.

But he could make sure she knew he was here, with her. He bit down on the nausea and reached out, capturing her hand in his. She glanced over at him, squeezing back – so weak but still, the trust, it hit him square in the chest, making it difficult to breathe.

Strong. So strong. Even in the face of the fear that threatened to rip up out of her and tear them all apart. She was strong enough to push down the fear, to keep her power at bay, no matter what it cost her.

Had he thought it necessary to show her what the Christmas spirit was about? He'd been an unthinking idiot. She was the one who could teach all of them its true meaning.

He squeezed her hand harder.

It seemed to give her strength. She took in a steadier breath and said, "I don't know why I didn't realise I was using Dawn's life-force energy. It wasn't obvious before. Now it is. But Loki showed me what I need to do." She glanced at Trip, her eyes warming a little as she met his gaze.

"And what is that?" Bas asked breathlessly.

Her mouth trembled and he saw how hard it was for her to go on, and yet she did. "Trip must drink my blood. Doing so will create a link between Trip and me that is stronger than the one I share with Dawn. The creation of that link will break my link with her, and she will be free. Once free of me, she will recover quickly."

"And you're willing to do this?" Korinna asked quietly. "Even though it's blood magic? Like what was done to you?"

She nodded firmly. "It will save Dawn. That's all that matters." Her hand tightened on Trip's, squeezing so hard, if he wasn't a God, it might have broken his fingers. But he didn't protest, just let her hold on.

If it was giving her strength and comfort, she could break every bone in that hand and the other if she needed to.

"Gods, Ilia. I'm so sorry you have to do this," Korinna said, voice breaking. "I wish there was another way."

Ilia turned to meet her friend's gaze. "There isn't. Loki showed us. This is the only way."

"You trust what he showed you?"

She nodded, and so did he. "There are things we need to share with you, but not now. Now, you need to bring Dawn in here so we can save her."

"Why does she have to be in here with you?" Bas asked.

"The vision Loki showed us. She was lying here." She moved into the middle of the bed and patted the spot beside her. "And Trip and I were on this side. I think we need to do it exactly as we saw it to make sure it works."

"Okay," Bas said. He disappeared from the room. Everything fell silent.

"Is there anything I can do?" Violetta said, hovering near the end of the bed next to Tamuel and Korinna. "Anything to make you more comfortable?"

"Can I have some water?" Ilia asked.

"Me too," Trip said. His mouth had already been dry when he woke, now it was also burning, and tasted disgusting. "Maybe some mint to chew on as well."

"I'll be right back," Violetta said, disappearing out the door, leaving them there with his daughter and her mate.

"Where are Daphne and the boys?" Trip asked.

"In their cottage. I spelled them to stay there until we managed to wake you. It was harder than I thought it would be, especially with Daphne and Gideon. I had to keep sending them both back. They were determined to check on you – and Gideon kept mentioning Christmas."

"They always spend it here with me."

"Well, maybe they still can, given you've woken on Christmas Eve."

Ilia gasped. "Almost two weeks have passed?"

"Loki did intimate that time was passing much faster

here than where he'd taken us to show us the past, present and future."

"But ... he also said she had until Christmas. Why did he keep us there so long? We're lucky she's not already dead. We have to do this now."

Bas and Jules hurried into the room, Dawn's limp body cradled in her mother's arms.

"Jules," Ilia said, voice breaking. "I'm so sorry."

Jules shook her head, tears tumbling down her face. "Don't be sorry. Just make it better."

Ilia nodded sharply and patted the bed. "Lay her here, head next to my shoulder."

Jules lowered Dawn, then with a whimper, knelt beside the bed, one hand on her daughter's head, the other holding her little hand.

"You have to let go and stand back," Ilia said.

Jules' lip wobbled as the tears fell harder. "I'm not sure I can."

"You have to. We have to do this exactly as we saw it," Trip said, voice gruff with emotion.

"Come on, Jules." Bas took her hands in his, helping her up from beside the bed, holding her trembling form to his even as a world of grief and pain chased across his face. "We have to trust they know what they're doing."

"I do," Jules said. "I know Ilia will do everything she can to save my baby."

Ilia's face twisted again before she managed a watery smile. "You trust me with her life?"

"Of course. Always."

"Thank you."

Jules leaned down and kissed Dawn on the forehead, then Ilia. "Bring her back to us."

"I will." She took a deep breath then lay down, still

holding Trip's hand. Then turning her head to meet his gaze, her astonishing eyes glowing in the dark, she said, "Do it now. Before I lose my grip on my fear."

He nodded, cupped her face and whispered, "I love you."

Then before he could even see how she might respond to that statement, he bent over her, his teeth elongating as Tamuel had said a God's teeth would for this very thing. Then, mouth suddenly watering, he bit into the sensitive, fragrant flesh of her neck.

CHAPTER

NINETEEN

I lia whimpered as Trip's new fangs sank into her neck – just like Tiberinus' had – slicing through her skin with hardly any resistance, piercing the artery that carried her life's blood through her body. But unlike with Tiberinus, she felt no fear, no revulsion.

Her entire world centred on those three little words he'd just uttered.

How could they carry such power?

But they did.

She felt them inside her, growing, feeding her soul as he fed from her life's blood.

He loved her.

It seemed improbable, and yet, she knew with a deep certainty, the like of which she'd never felt before, that he did.

He loved her.

And she loved him.

Maybe it was the soul-bond that Loki had talked about, forcing them to love each other. But she didn't think that was it. There was no feeling of being forced.

Only a huge sense of freedom. Like she was a bird who'd had her wings clipped but was suddenly able to fly.

That sense of freedom, it had started with lust, certainly, creating sensations in her body that made her feel more like herself than she ever had. That lust had been true. She had trusted it. And that trust had grown, fed by Trip's trust in her, his belief that she was good.

It was then solidified by the realisation that he wasn't the only one who felt that.

The people around her – her family, if not by blood, then by choice – all believed in her too. They believed in her goodness; had been trying to make her be true to that all these months as they'd shown their love and support and tried to enfold her into their family and make her feel like she belonged. They'd trusted her with the task of finding Trip. They'd trusted her enough to start to train her how to use and control her new magic.

But the best thing of all – to use a metaphor suitable to this time of the year – the thing that had turned a lonely, damaged pine tree into a true representation of Christmas spirit was that they believed in her enough to save Dawn. To do exactly as she asked and stand back and let her do it.

That trust, added to Trip's – it was everything she'd never had and more. It filled her up inside and made her glow, not with fury and fear, but with love and happiness, and yes, Christmas spirit.

Joy. She felt joyous.

She'd never in her life felt joyous before. And it was the most marvellous sensation.

"Look, she's glowing all over," someone said reverently.

"The link. Between Dawn and Ilia. Can anyone else see it?"

"It's getting weaker."

"Where's the one between Trip and Ilia?" That was Korinna, her voice worried. "I thought they said that was supposed to appear to take its place."

"What happens if it doesn't?" Jules sounded worried.

"She'll die." Bas whispered. "She needs a life-force to help keep her alive until we find another solution. It's why we just couldn't break the link between her and Dawn."

He was right. She knew that now. Knew this was why Loki hadn't been able to show her any more of her future – she didn't have one. But that thought wasn't enough to mute her joy.

"What can we do?" Tamuel's pained question did, stabbing her in the heart.

"Nothing," she whispered to them. "You can do nothing. My life doesn't matter. Only Dawn's."

Trip lifted his head, his hand convulsing against her cheek, his tortured gaze meeting hers. "Your life does matter."

She touched his lip, his fang. "You must keep drinking."

"Not if it will take your life."

"You must. I give it willingly. For you. For Dawn. It's necessary. To save you all."

"No. I won't. It's not fair."

"A life for a life. It's the penalty we must pay. I've had more than my fair share, anyway. Drink. Before it's too late."

"Ilia," Jules said, bursting into tears.

She reached out her hand for Jules to take. "It's okay. These last months have been a gift I never thought to have. To be a part of your family." She turned back to face Trip. "To know love. True love. I leave you all far happier than I have ever been." She took Trip's head in her hands. He was still so weak from their trip to the in-between that it was easy to guide his head back to her neck. "Drink, my love. Let your touch be the last thing I feel."

"No," Trip moaned against her neck even as his fangs sank into her skin once more, as if the Fates and destiny were too strong for him to fight against. Another sign this was meant to be.

"I don't want to lose you. I can't lose you," she heard in her head. Trip, somehow talking through the soul-bond as he drank. *"Not now I've found you."*

"I will always be with you," she whispered.

"Not how I want. Not how you deserve. The Gods ask too much of you. This was supposed to be a giving and a taking. A sharing. Now it's just all give from you and all take from me." As the words echoed in her head, he sucked harder, groaning against her skin as if the action pained him.

But she felt no pain. All she felt was rightness and a need. A need that was growing inside her. A need for the sharing he was talking about. A need for his life-force to be in her.

A need for ... his blood.

As the thought hit her, fangs grew in her mouth, pricking her lower lip.

What? How? She wasn't a Goddess.

"Maybe not," a distinctly female voice whispered in her head. *"But you are Trip's soul-bound mate, equal to him in every way. Be equal now. The sharing is a two-way street."*

Oh!

Sharing. That's what this was truly meant to be. While he drank of her blood, she was supposed to complete the circuit by drinking of his.

But with him at her neck, how could she do it?

His fingers convulsed against her face, his wrist

brushing up next to her mouth. Without thought, she turned and sank her new fangs into his skin.

The copper tang of blood rushed into her mouth followed by a rush of power and a scent that was like apples and summer fruit and the blooms that had grown in the garden he'd made with his blood. It filled her, making everything inside her grow and reform, settling into something new.

Something that was just her.

Something that was part of him too. But not in a cloying way. Not in a way that made her feel trapped. No. This was like when he'd told her he loved her, like when she realised she was part of a family, like when she realised she loved him, and felt freed by it.

And as that sense of freedom swept through her, there was a wrenching tear as the link binding her to Dawn snapped. But that tear didn't remain an open wound. It healed immediately, the frayed ends of the bond reaching, stretching, joining.

With him. With her love. With Trip.

He was hers and she was his and together they were flying to a freedom she never thought to have.

Somewhere in the distance, a baby wailed, accompanied by shouts of joy. Movement beside her as the slight weight of Dawn was lifted from the bed. She rolled over, closer into Trip, her arms tightening around him, her leg sliding over his as they twined together, both taking, both giving.

They were one.

And it was the most magnificent thing in the entire universe.

In her eyes, stars swirled faster and faster until they

exploded, a magnificent firework, and she and Trip were falling, falling, right into each other's arms.

~

SHE AWOKE SOMETIME LATER to the sound of carols drifting through the closed door, along with talking, laughter and the tearing of paper.

Trip shifted, mumbling something about sweetness and light, then rolled over onto his back. She made a sound of protest in her throat – she wasn't ready to let go of him yet, to let go of the warmth, the feeling of completion – but then he pulled her to him, her head nestled on the firmness of his broad chest, hand over his heart.

A heart that beat in time with hers; a heart that pumped with her blood alongside his, as hers pumped his blood alongside hers; a heart that now held her deep inside.

She'd been so stupid to hold herself back from this; to let old fear rule her so completely. But now none of that mattered because she was home.

"That's nice," she muttered.

"What?" he murmured, moving his hand to brush her hair back from her face and tip up her chin.

She opened her eyes to see his, the light green glowing in the dark and filled with his love for her. His trust in her. His happiness in her. She smiled up at him. "This. Being here like this. It feels like home."

"It does. Being with you will always feel like that for me now. I love you."

"I love you too."

He bent down as she reached up, their lips meeting in a soft, longing kiss. She would have deepened it, but the sounds from outside the door got louder and he pulled away. "We better not," he said softly. "They might come through that door to check on us at any moment."

She nodded. She didn't want to get caught making love to him; the first time they truly made love, she wanted it to be just them, so she could lose herself in him completely.

She settled beside him, both turned on their sides, staring into each other's eyes.

She still couldn't believe this had happened; that after everything, she'd found her soulmate, had tied herself to him in every conceivable way and was filled with light and joy because of it.

For the first time in her life, she was peaceful. Next to realising she was in love with Trip and the magnificence of sharing blood with him, it was the most remarkable feeling she'd ever experienced.

"Should we go out and join them? Let them know we're awake? Sounds like it's Christmas morning with all the paper tearing."

"Can we just stay here a little longer?" she asked.

"Sounds perfect to me." He touched beside her eyes, the longing and love in his warming all the places inside her that had been so cold for so long. "Beautiful. So beautiful," he whispered as he ran his finger over her brow, down her nose and along her cheek.

"So are you." She mirrored his gesture. "Your eyes are glowing."

"Are they? So are yours. Like sunlight over a mountain peak at dawn, all purple and golden. In fact, all of you is glowing."

It was then she realised that the light she could see his face by was coming from her. She looked down at herself. Trip was right. She *was* glowing. But it wasn't the worrisome glow that had emanated from her chest because of her fury. This was like after Dawn had turned her spirit form into a corporeal one at Easter. Except the light was more silvery than golden.

It was kind of pretty except ... She growled deep in her chest. "Damn it. Not again!" It had taken a few months for that glow to dim enough so that she could go outside and not be subject to people's stares.

"You look like an angel. Like you'd be more at home perched at the top of a Christmas tree."

She growled louder. "Not funny." She sat up slowly, a little stiff but surprisingly okay for someone who'd been close to death not so long ago. "I am nothing close to an angel. I'm a thing of broken edges and angles. I'm a mess." She went to tuck her hair behind her ear, then stopped as her fingers tangled in the rat's nest of knots and mess that had taken up residence on the side she'd been lying on. "Agh! Look at my hair! Actually, don't look at it!" She quickly tried to smooth it down, but stopped when he chuckled and replaced her hands with his.

"You are beautiful as you are, mess and all. I'm not exactly perfect either."

"But you're a God – or something like one."

"Given you drank my blood like that, so must you be."

She grimaced. "I don't know how."

"Don't you?" He waved his hand at her chest. "You spent thousands of years in a piece of a Goddess' heart. Then you were remade with Goddess-gifted energy. You, like me, have had more than one Goddess' power responsible for remaking what you are now. Huh ... I wonder what those two Goddesses powers mixed together in one powerful witch could turn into? Do you think—"

She put her fingers against his lips, uninterested in the

latter part of his musings. "You remember where you came from?"

He sat up beside her, grasping her hands in his, sliding his thumbs over the pulse point in her wrists. "Yes. Much is still foggy, but I can remember where I came from. I can remember Demeter and Persephone and Gaia. I can remember first hearing the prophecy and about Perses. I remember coming up with the idea to create the Eleusinian Mysteries to help others fight the coming darkness; the changes I made to it to help my daughter after I found out Innia was pregnant." He swallowed hard. "I remember what it felt like to leave Innia, pregnant with Korinna, how it felt to know I might never know my daughter or see the woman I loved again."

"Oh. Trip."

He smiled softly at her. "It's an old pain, one that barely hurts now I know you. What I felt for Innia – it was a young love, never having time to mature. What I feel for you however is deeper and so much more encompassing. I will always love Innia, but that love is nothing to what I feel for you."

"I know," she said softly, brushing his hair from his forehead. "I know. And I am glad you remember her." She blinked tears from her eyes.

"As am I."

"It is not too much? Remembering all of it?"

He tipped his head. "I remember only a small portion as yet. I think that's as it must be. I don't think it would be comfortable to have everything come rushing back all at once."

"Do you think we might need to drink each other's blood again? To gain back your memories completely?"

He tipped his head to the side, looking warily at her. "Will you mind if we do?"

She glance down at their linked hands, chewing on her lip – careful not to break the skin with her newly pointy eye-teeth – as if she was considering it.

"It's okay if you don't. I'm sure they will come back eventually with what we've shared. I can already feel them at the back of my mind, like a cloud of fog just waiting to clear."

She looked up at him through her eyelashes, unable to hold back the mischievous smile. "I think I might be able to handle it. As long as we get to do it in a private place with nobody watching on, because next time we do, I'm not going to be able to stop from jumping your bones."

His mouth wobbled as he tried to hold back his smile. "I could get on board with that."

"Good." A noise from the lounge room made her glance at the door. "I wish we were alone now."

"So do I. But we're not. Although," he frowned a little. "I think I remember how to whisk us away to somewhere private if that's what you wish."

"You would do that for me? Miss out on your precious Christmas morning with your daughter and her family – the first Christmas you've ever shared with her?"

"I would. In a heartbeat. There will be other Christmases. But there won't be another first morning that I wake with you in my arms. And making love to you now would be the best Christmas gift I've ever given or received."

Her lips quirked. "Oh really? You think it would be the best Christmas gift you could give to me? Got tickets on yourself, I see."

"With what I'm remembering I can do, you bet."

He lunged and she laughed as his arms wrapped around

her, taking her down to the bed, their lips meeting in a kiss that was all tongue and tasting and passion. She felt him deep inside her, but she wanted even more. She'd always want more. But could she ask him to give up his precious Christmas after everything they'd been through?

No, she couldn't. Couldn't do that to him, or to herself.She wanted to share this Christmas with him and everyone out there too.

The shock of that realisation had her gasping.

He pulled back. "What is it?"

CHAPTER

TWENTY

Before she could answer, the door banged open and they looked up as a body shot across the room to bounce on the end of the bed. "Trip! You're awake."

"Gideon! Come back here." Daphne appeared in the doorway.

More bouncing as Gideon shouted, "He's awake! I said I could hear him talking."

"Stop that. They don't need you bouncing on the bed!" Daphne entered the room, obviously with the intent to grab her youngest son.

Before she could, Trip pulled Gideon to him, giving him a hug and ruffling his hair. "It's fine. I'm used to this rascal bouncing on my bed first thing Christmas morning. It's a tradition."

"Dad?" The question had him looking up as Korinna entered the room. The others appeared in the doorway behind her, delight and relief in their eyes and smiles. Korinna edged closer, hands wringing in front of her, Tamuel at her back. "Do you ... do you remember?"

"Oh, my dear. My darling girl. I'm sorry. I'm so sorry I

left you and your mother like I did. But I had no choice. I hope you understand I had no choice?"

"I do. I do!" She rushed to him, hands stretched to take his. Gideon moved so Trip could pull her close, enfolding her in his arms. "Dad. Dad. You remember? You remember."

A lump rose in Ilia's throat, her chin wobbling as she blinked back threatening tears.

"Not everything. But it's coming back." Trip kissed his daughter's head, holding her close for a moment before pulling away to look down at her. "It's all coming back." He reached out to grab Ilia's hand while holding Korinna to his side in a hug. "Ilia and I will share more blood to make certain I get all of my memories back."

"You will?" Korinna asked, gaze flying to Ilia's.

Ilia nodded. "Of course. It's the least I can do after all you've done for me. Besides ..." She shared a secret smile with Trip. "It wasn't as bad as I thought."

"That's such a relief," Jules said, as she came to the other side of the bed, Dawn in her arms.

"Oh!" Ilia said, gaze raking over the baby. "She looks so well. As if nothing ever happened."

Dawn held her arms out, leaning towards Ilia. Jules handed her over. Ilia hugged the baby to her, kissing her downy head, breathing in the smell that was baby powder and fresh soap with a hint of lavender and something else that was all Dawn. "I'm so glad you're okay, Dawny. So very glad."

Dawn placed her hand on the side of Ilia's face. In her mind she heard, *"I'm happy you well now too."*

"What?" She blinked, uncertain if she'd imagined what she thought she'd just heard.

"It'th me!" Dawn smiled brightly.

"That's ... that's impossible!" Their communication had

always been in images and feelings, never words. Dawn was too young for anything else.

"She spoke to you?"

Her gaze snapped to Jules. "What?" She glanced around as the others all nodded. They'd heard her too. "How? Mind speech at such a young age is unheard of."

Jules shrugged. "It seems that in separating from you, her powers have grown. She can now speak to us all if she touches us. Bas thinks she'll be able to do it soon without even having to do that. Some form of Goddessly mind-speak she inherited from Ostara."

"That's ... amazing?"

Jules' mouth twisted into something that wasn't quite a smile. "We'll see." She shared a worried look with Bas. Ilia couldn't blame her. This was just one more thing to make the Gods look Dawn's way – and that wasn't something anyone wanted. They'd all suffered from too much attention from the Gods and Goddesses in the past. Yet it seemed that the Eternal Well wasn't done with them.

Even if she hadn't already made up her mind to stay and help, she wouldn't be going anywhere now. She couldn't leave Jules and Bas and the others to deal with any of this alone.

Nothing could make her leave the family she'd found.

Trip gripped her hand tightly, as if he could feel what she was thinking, and when she met his gaze, he said, "I'm glad you feel that way. So do I."

She nodded. Neither of them were ever leaving their family again.

"I guess that means I'm bequeathing the farm early to Daphne and her boys."

"What? No. You can't!" Daphne said, putting her arms

around Gideon as he bounced to the foot of the bed, Charlie and Harry coming to stand behind her.

"Of course I can. It was going to be yours anyway when I left. It's just going to be a few years early."

"What do you mean you're leaving and it was going to be mine anyway? Does this have something to do with you being a God?"

Trip gasped, his gaze flying to Korinna and Tamuel.

Tamuel shrugged. "We had to tell them. Our spells didn't work on them for long – on Daphne and Gideon not at all for some reason. They came in after you and Ilia started the blood magic and saw it all – bit hard to hide, given it whipped up a magical storm of light that flowed out of the house brighter than your Christmas lights."

He stared at Daphne and the boys. "You're … you're okay with it?"

"It's fantastic! I always thought you were like Santa but this is even better," Gideon enthused from his place at the end of the bed.

Daphne's arms tightened around Gideon as she smiled at Trip and Ilia. "It explains a lot."

He looked to the other boys, his hand tightening around Ilia's as he waited.

Harry nodded slowly then smiled and said, "Gideon's right. It's super cool."

Charlie's smile was a bit slower. "Will I be able to grow the trees without you?"

Trip blew out a breath. "Of course you will."

"So, no Godly powers were used in the making of this farm," Charlie said, lips quirking a little.

Trip chuckled. "No. Well, maybe the trees won't grow quite as fast. That was a magic I couldn't seem to help using. But I've shared with you all my growing tips. You are more than capable of keeping this place going – if you want to?"

"I want to," Charlie said. "I love working the land." He glanced down and then back up again. "It's something I learned from you."

"You won't go and never come back though, will you?" Gideon asked, eyes shadowed.

Trip glanced at Ilia, his eyes asking her what she thought.

His sharing of this decision filled her with happiness. "We can come back as often as you want. As often as they need you. They're your family too. I wouldn't ask you to abandon them. And maybe, after we've finished all this, we can come back and live here."

"Really?"

"Of course. I mean, it's not like Korinna and the others can't just open a portal and visit at any time. So, we'd all still be together."

He smiled wildly, cupped her face and gave her a smacking kiss.

Tamuel wolf-whistled.

Korinna said, "I'd say get a bed, but you already have one."

Bas suggested, "Maybe we should leave them to it."

Ilia pulled back from the kiss and, smiling said, "No way. We've got Christmas presents to unwrap! And a feast to prepare and eat."

"You want to stay for Christmas?" Trip asked, eyes wide.

"My first proper Christmas? I can't think of a better place to spend it or better people to spend it with."

Trip leaned in to give her another kiss. Then, leaning back a little, hands still cupping her face, he said, "Loki was so wrong. I knew you'd get this Christmas spirit thing!"

She smiled crookedly at him. "Christmas with a family like ours ... what's not to love?" There would never be anymore bah-humbugs from her.

She dragged him up and out of the bed to lead everyone out of the bedroom and into the sunlit lounge where a huge Christmas tree sat in the corner, twinkling at them.

Everyone gasped as they entered the room. A truckload of presents had appeared under and around the tree, crushing the few that hadn't already been opened.

"What the Hells?"

"Where did they come from?"

Ilia raised her brows at Trip and he shook his head, as baffled as the rest of them.

Gideon whooped and dived in to the pile as Daphne said, "A Christmas miracle."

Ilia leaned in to Trip, loving how his arm went around her shoulders so naturally, tucking her into his side. "You're my Christmas miracle," she said, looking up at him.

"And you're mine." He kissed her lightly before he was pulled forward by Harry who, even though usually evincing teenage cool, couldn't keep his enthusiasm at bay.

The next few hours were spent opening presents – there were some for everyone in the miracle pile – clearing the torn wrapping paper and find places for all the gifts so they could bring in the trestle tables and start to load them up with the Christmas feast that Daphne, Jules, Bas and Tamuel were creating in the kitchen.

Ilia had never laughed so much as she worked. She sang carols with everyone as they tidied up – even though she didn't know most of the words – and rearranged the furniture and set the table. At least, she did when she wasn't being waylaid by Trip every few minutes – he seemed to feel the need to touch and kiss her as much as she did him.

When they sat down to the meal, Trip raised his glass to give a toast, but Ilia put her hand on top of his, stopping him, and stood. All eyes went to her.

"I just wanted to say, I thought Christmas was stupid and the idea of the Christmas spirit even worse. I thought it was all about taking and wanting – kind of a reflection of my life before I was freed from the HeartsBlood Gem."

She swallowed, eyes pricking with tears as she looked around at all of their dear faces. "But you have all shown me over the last year or so I've been around you all, first in the HeartsBlood Gem and then in this corporeal form, what friendship and family and love truly is. You gave me your trust and never asked for anything from me I wasn't willing to give. Even then, I was still wary of how I could ever be a part of something so good. I felt so broken and angry and cold."

Her gaze landed on Dawn, sitting in a high chair that Daphne had grabbed out of the storage shed. "But a little baby, full of dawn's light of renewal, started warming my heart and then all of you crept in with her, starting to heal my heart and soul in a way I never thought I wanted or deserved. Because of that, I was ready to open myself up to trust and believe when I finally met the man we'd all been looking for; the man who is the other part of my soul." She smiled at him, then at everyone at the table. "Thank you for sticking by me and sticking with me and never giving up on me, even when I had given up on myself. You helped to lead me here, to this moment, and I will be forever grateful. May the Eternal Well guide you and keep you safe and help us as we face what is coming. Together."

They all stood, raising their glasses. "Together."

They drank and as they did, there was a rolling knock in the distance – the Eternal Well accepting their vow to fight together to defeat the rising tide of evil that was Perses.

Ilia's gaze met Trip's – and instead of feeling worried at another vow having been made, she felt strengthened by it.

Like Demeter's vow to get Trip back, this one would work too.

How could it not when they were not only all working as one towards a common goal, but had the bonds of love and family and friendship to strengthen them and carry them through?

"We'll win the day," Trip whispered to her.

"We will."

Then they proceeded to have the merriest of merry Christmases.

EPILOGUE

"That was nice of you to give them all those gifts. Especially given Christmas is hardly part of your pantheon's religion."

Loki turned to see Demeter come up behind him, then looked back at the glimmering mirror he watched Trip and Ilia through. "After years of watching Trip and nudging him along, I kind of see the appeal."

He frowned as Trip started talking to an empty chair at the table next to him. "I'm a little worried though that I broke him. He seems to be talking to imaginary people." He pointed to Ilia who was also talking to the empty chair beside her. "I think I might have broken her too. Does drinking blood lead to some kind of madness for their kind?"

Demeter sighed. "I suppose it's time." She waved her hand over the image. At first, nothing happened, then there was a wavering in the spaces where he had seen nothing but empty chairs.

As the wavering clarified, he leaned forward. "Fuck me! No. It can't be." He stared at the woman who'd appeared in the chair next to Trip. It looked like her but ... it couldn't be. She was long lost to him. "Have I gone mad too? Did I spend too long in the in-between?"

"No. You're not going mad. It's her."

He glanced at Demeter to see sad resignation in her eyes, but then couldn't stop his gaze from being drawn back to the woman in the image. "Callie?"

"Yes. Your Callianthe. Although, she's called Daphne now."

"But ... how? She died. Zeus killed her. He came after her and the boys after he killed her adoptive family." She and the boys had been punished for King Lycaon's hubris - who he hoped was still being tortured in Tartarus.

"No. He didn't. I found her and saved her. She was supposed to die alongside her sisters and their people, but I couldn't allow it. She was needed. So I warped her fate and brought her and her children to this time."

"What? Why?"

"She and the boys are important to the fight ahead. Besides, you would never have become what you needed to become if she'd stayed."

His mind reeling, he stumbled back from the vision. "I have to go to her." He raised his hand to call a portal, but Demeter stepped in front of him. His magic died with a little puff.

"You cannot go to her. Not yet. There are things to do. For you and for her."

"No. I have to go!"

She stopped him from moving past her, her grip firmer than it had any right to be – damn she was strong! "She is not ready to remember you yet. It will endanger her and the boys. And your child."

"My child?"

He looked back at the image, at the three boys who had appeared in the other previously empty seats at the table. Two of them he recognised as the children she had borne by the man her father had tied her to. A man long dead, killed in the raid that had brought Callianthe to Loki's attention. The boys were only ten or so years older than when he'd last seen them. How could that be? It had been thousands of years.

But the question didn't get asked of Demeter, because his eyes landed on the youngest one.

The boy's eyes were a startling, spring green and his hair was dark as night. There was also the whisper of sharp cheekbones and pointed chin that would be identical to his one day.

"My son?"

Demeter's hand landed on his shoulder. "Yes."

He had a son! A roar of need burst to life inside him. "How could you have kept this from me?"

"I had to."

Anger, pain, loss, confusion rushed through him to be pushed aside by one overwhelming need. "I have to go to them."

"No. It isn't time."

"I don't care. I have to go."

He struggled against her grip, lifted his hands to use his magic, but it was a useless gesture in this place that was hers, filled with her magic, giving her dominion over all who stood here with her.

She whispered a word, and his magic fizzled out.

"Loki. I'm sorry. I know you want to go to them, but you can't. Not yet. It isn't time. I wasn't lying when I said it would endanger them. Besides, they won't accept you. She won't even remember you."

"What do you mean?"

"I took her memory too when I placed her here, replaced it, and the older boys' memories, with a different past to remember. I did this so she would not grieve for you and all she'd lost. But also so that she could be a help to Trip. To be family for him. He needed that so he could be ready for Ilia."

"Why didn't you tell me!"

"I couldn't do that either. You had to live your life thinking she was gone. And for all intents and purposes, she has been, until now."

There was so much she wasn't telling him, he could tell, but he was so confused - so happy and yet kind of numb at the same time - that he couldn't think straight enough to form the questions scrabbling in his brain. "Break the spell. Let them remember."

She gripped both his shoulders and looked deeply into his eyes. "You are like my son, Loki, and I love you, but if you try to go to her now and ruin everything we've worked towards, I will smite you down without hesitation."

He shivered, seeing in her eyes her determination that would let nothing – not even her love for him or Trip or Persephone or even the long dead Innia – to get in the way of stopping Perses from coming back into the living Realms. She was right. He too had thought he would never let anything get in the way of that goal. But this ...

He closed his eyes, shutting out the sight of his love, her boys, his son. "How long?" he finally managed to ask.

"Not long in the scheme of things. Ilia and Trip have a bit more work to do to solidify their bond and be able to use their magic side by side to strengthen everything Trip and Korinna must do. There is also the issue of Dawn's growth and training. Once we have taken care of those issues, you will be able to go to Callie and remind her of what you once were to each other."

"She will remember me then?"

Demeter nodded. "The spell on her is not the one I placed on Trip. It is far less severe. She will remember when the Fates align and she is ready. Then you will go to her and your son. You will train him as I trained you and he will help in the fight ahead."

"But he is so young."

She pointed at the image, at the baby in her highchair. "If that baby can help, your son is not too young."

"You ask a lot."

"I know. But it is necessary." Her eyes blanked as she stared off into a future he couldn't see. "Once all the threads I have woven are in place, you will all see the bigger picture and you will know what I know. That only united by the heart's curse, can we beat back the evil that is coming."

"The heart's curse?"

She nodded. "Love."

He frowned at her. "Love is not a curse."

She smiled, the expression nothing comforting. "To Perses, it will be the greatest curse of them all."

I HOPE you enjoyed this first part of Trip and Ilia's story. There will be more to come with *Fates Cursed: Gods Cursed Series Book 5.*

I have a bonus NSFW sexy epilogue that I wrote for you to finish off this part of their story, but before I get to that, I have a little sneak peek of the first few chapters of *Fates Cursed* right here. Just turn the page …

FATES CURSED

GODS CURSED: BOOK 5

CHAPTER
ONE

"Is she asleep?" Korinna asked Jules as she entered the kitchen, Ilia following close behind.

Jules nodded as she joined Korinna at the kitchen table then looked back at Ilia who stood behind her. "Thanks to Ilia."

"No thanks necessary." Ilia patted Jules on the shoulder. "Just doing what I can to help." She gestured at the pot of tea Korinna had in her hand. "I'd love a cuppa though. Should I put the kettle on?"

"Don't bother. This pot is fresh. It's Violetta's relaxation blend. I thought you might need it to help you sleep." She checked the clock on the wall behind her. "It's only just after midnight so we could all still get a decent night's sleep with a little help." She began to pour it into the mugs that were already on the table.

"You're a Goddess," Jules said, reaching for one. "I'm so tired." She gave Ilia a gimlet stare as the ancient witch took a seat next to her. "I'm not quite sure why you're not given you're up every night helping me with my baby girl." She put one of the steaming mugs in front of Ilia. "What's your secret?"

Ilia shrugged as she picked it up and cupped it in her hands. She was exhausted, but not because her sleep was constantly interrupted by little Dawn's nightmares. It had more to do with the fact Trip, her soulmate, couldn't keep his hands off her, just as she couldn't keep hers off him. Every night was filled with the kind of glorious lovemaking she'd never known was possible. If not for how it filled her with energy, particularly when their fangs grew and they shared in each other's blood as Trip pounded into her in the way she needed him to, she would probably be worse off than Jules.

Although, if Trip stayed away any longer in his search for Loki, she was going to be in trouble. The sexual energy from their last encounter a week ago had been waning over the last day or so.

But she didn't say any of that. She simply followed up the shrug with an, "I have no idea."

She lifted her mug to her nose and took in a deep breath. The fragrant scent of jasmine, chamomile and a hint of lavender flowed around her, soothing her as much as the warmth from the tea-heated ceramic.

"Perhaps we're all used to a lack of sleep," Korinna said, her eyes dancing as she lifted her cup and blew across the hot liquid. "I don't know about you, but Tamuel keeps me up most nights." She waggled her brows. "In the best way."

Jules snorted. "I'm not sure I should hear that about my soul-son."

"It's no worse than him hearing you and Bas testing the springs on your bed every night. Or the way sexually tinged power zaps through the air every time Ilia and my dad are at it." Korinna shuddered dramatically

"What?" Ilia's mug thunked down on the table, tea splashing over the rim. "That does not happen! You're making that up."

"I'm afraid I'm not." Korinna laughed. "You should see your face!"

Horrified, Ilia turned to Jules for confirmation.

Jules chuckled. "Umm, I have to admit what Korinna said is 100% true."

Ilia's cheeks heated – and the rest of her along with it. Hades' balls. She wanted to sink under the table and never be seen again. Gaze firmly on the liquid in her mug she said, "Hells, I'm so sorry. I had no idea."

Jule's snort of laughter had her looking up.

"Don't be sorry," the other witch said, patting her hand. "The sex after your energy hits us is even better. Bas already had stamina, but now ..." She waved her hand in front of her face. "It's spectacular."

"Oh Hells!" Ilia said, dropping her head into her hands. Then a thought hit and her head whipped up, gaze searching Korinna's smirking face. "That doesn't happen to you and Tam, does it?"

Korinna grimaced comically and said, "Yep."

"Argh! This is beyond embarrassing," she wailed, hiding her face in her hands again. Gods damn it! It wasn't only embarrassing. It was wrong.

Korinna might be over 2000 years old and only recently had found, and was getting to know, her father, but his sex life really wasn't something she needed to know anything about. Especially if said sex life was creating a situation that affected her and her mate in a way that made them horny. Not that they really needed help in that department – she'd spent months with them when she was in the HeartsBlood Gem and embedded in Tam's chest to keep her close and safe. She'd had to shut off her awareness many, many times while Korinna and Tam were having sexy-times after they mated.

But still ... She lifted her head and forced herself to look at her daughter-in-law. "You shouldn't be pushed into having sex because of something your father and I are doing. That must be so ... scarring."

Korinna snorted. "In the scheme of my life, not really."

Ilia couldn't stop her chin from wobbling as tears pricked her eyes. "I'm so sorry. I didn't mean to make things worse for you."

Korinna leaned forward and grabbed Ilia's wrist. "Please don't be sorry. Honestly, it's not that bad. Sure, it was a bit uncomfortable at first, knowing where the energy was coming from and why, but now ..." A smile blossomed on her lips and her eyes turned a little dreamy. "I knew Tam was creative but ..." She coughed a little and came back to herself. "Jules is right. Something about what you're both putting out there makes things even better. It's like he's in me spiritually as I'm in him and it's even more than the mating bond and yet it *is* the mating bond." She waved her hand, frowning in consternation. "I'm not explaining it very well."

"I think you're explaining it exactly right," Jules said as she leaned over to pat Ilia's hand. "We're not worried about it and you shouldn't be either."

Ilia grimaced. "I'm not sure about that. And I don't think Trip will be when I tell him." She knew he'd be as horrified as she was. "I knew we shouldn't have stayed." She stood up, her chair screeching across the parquetry. "As soon as Trip comes back, we'll go."

"No!" Korinna and Jules shouted at the same time.

Ilia looked between them in surprise. "But ... we've been

here for months and we always intended to find a place nearby or go back to Trip's farm." The only reason they hadn't was because Trip needed to be where Korinna was after having chosen to have his memory wiped and be separated from his unborn daughter to safeguard her. Now he had his memories back and was recently reunited with her well ... There was so much he wanted to know about her; so much he wanted to make up for.

And Ilia hadn't argued the point because, apart from feeling his need, she felt her own need to be close to Dawn. Despite the spell at Christmas she and Trip had performed that separated her life-force from Dawn's and saved both hers and the baby's lives, the need to be around the growing toddler hadn't abated. In fact, it had grown as Dawn had grown – growth that wasn't normal physically or mentally. Not only had Dawn's ability to use mind-speech increased, her powers were beginning to manifest strongly – unusual in someone so young – and she was growing physically much faster than she should.

If one counted things as the humans did, she was about to turn one – her birthday was in two days' time – but she was about the size of a three-year-old and had the mental capacity of a child a few years older still. And every time she had one of her fits at night – seizures that gripped her entire body and filled her mind with nightmares that spilled out into all of them through her mind-speech ability – she aged a little faster.

Yesterday she'd been about average height and weight for a two-year-old but now ...

She shook her head and took a sip of tea, not caring that it was still too hot. It scalded her tongue, but she swallowed it down and took another. The fleeting pain was nothing to what poor little Dawn endured too many nights.

As if Korinna could read her mind, she placed her cup on the table then took Ilia's hand in hers. "We need you here." Her gaze flickered to Jules, who nodded. "Not just because you seem to be able to help Dawn come down from one of her fits faster than the rest of us can, but you are family."

"Not all families live in each other's pockets."

"This one does," Jules said. "We are stronger together. And as to you being embarrassed over the sexual power that you and Trip spill out into the world ... you don't need to be. I think it's happening for a reason."

"Why do you say that?" Ilia asked, frowning.

"Because everything has. Every event that has occurred since Bas came into my first incarnation's life has led to something necessary. And while you and Trip might be horrified that your sex life is affecting all of us, it's also strengthening us. It's creating tighter bonds between us and our soulmates."

"But how can that be?" The mating bond was unbreakable by anything but death – and came only second in strength and power to a soul-bond. Which was what Jules and Bas, and Korinna and Tam, and she and Trip all had.

Jules shrugged. "I know it seems an impossibility, but it's true."

Korinna nodded. "It is. And I think Jules is right. It's important. Besides ..." She ran her finger around the rim of her mug, "I need my Dad here. Plus over the last year, you've become more than a friend and family member, so I can't do without you close by either. But it's more than that." Her eyes lifted to meet Ilia's and something shifted in their depths. Her voice deepened as she said, "It's not only blood that binds and strengthens us."

Ilia shivered as the words echoed through her mind.

There was the touch of ancient power in Korinna's voice that pierced right into her very soul and made her new-found powers sit up and listen. If Korinna was right, she and Trip couldn't leave. And ... aside from that, she really didn't want to go – which was kind of surprising given how she used to feel about family and losing those she loved.

Slowly, she took a sip of her tea, swallowed and then voiced the thing that had been worrying her the last few days. "But ... what if it's me? What if my presence is making Dawn worse?"

Jules' and Korinna's eyes went wide and they looked at each other briefly before they both started shaking their heads. "Are you crazy?" Korinna asked.

"Maybe." Ilia looked down at her mug again and said softly, "But it wouldn't be the first time my presence was bad for her. I almost killed her last Christmas."

"You kept her alive last Christmas, despite the danger to yourself," Jules said, reaching across the table to grasp Ilia's hand. "Your energy has never been anything but positive towards Dawn."

"But how can you be certain?" she said, looking up into her friend's eyes. "We don't even know how my power works or where it truly came from. How can you be certain it's not made to hurt rather than heal?"

"Because, you've done nothing but help since you came to us. And Dawn loves you. She trusts you. She asks for you. She needs you. I don't think any of that would be true if you were the cause of whatever is happening to her."

"Jules is right," Korinna said, reaching to grasp her wrist and squeeze gently. "You always make Dawn better. There is no way you are causing Dawn's nightmares or her strange growth. That is something else entirely."

"But what?"

Korinna shrugged. "I don't know." She glanced at Jules then back again. "But I don't think we will discover what it is if you leave. I feel like you are essential to helping her. So you have to stay. Okay?"

Ilia met Korinna's firm gaze, then looked at Jules whose eyes pleaded with her. Tears swam in her vision and she looked down, covering the emotion. After a moment she said on a rasp, "Okay. We'll stay."

A loud sigh erupted from Jules as Korinna said, "Good."

Ilia glanced up to see the two women smiling at her in obvious relief. She began to return their smiles until a horrible thought hit her. "You don't think Dawn is being affected by Trip and me ... you know? Maybe her fits are being caused by—"

Korinna squeezed her hand again. "There is no correlation. Tam and I have already looked into that."

"You have?"

She nodded. "It wasn't hard to put together. You and Dad are blood-sharing most nights, right?"

Ilia blushed at the fact Korinna knew that, but nodded. "Yes. It feels ... necessary."

"Right. That's because it is." She waved her hand to forestall any questions that popped into Ilia's head. "We can go into that later. Right now, you need to know that what you and Dad are doing is not affecting Dawn at all."

"But how do you know for certain?"

"Simple. She's not having her fits every night," Jules said, getting up to fetch the biscuit jar from the counter behind them.

"That's not conclusive proof though. It could be building up in her until she has a fit."

"I don't think it is," Korinna said. "I mean, look at tonight."

"What about it?"

"Dad and Bas and Tam have been away for a week now searching for Loki to try and get some answers, so there's been no sexy times going on – for any of us."

She was more than aware of Trip's absence, the ache inside only assuaged by the fact she could feel their bond so strong and warm inside her – and the multiple face-time sessions a day because neither of them seemed to be able to go more than a few hours without seeing the other's face or hearing their voice.

Ugh, she'd never thought she'd be so pathetic and yet ... it was the most wonderful thing in her life. But that was beside the point. She pulled her thoughts back to their conversation. "Ah, I get your point. With Trip gone this last week there's been no special power leaking through the house. Yet Dawn's had some of her worst fits this week."

"Correct." Korinna nodded, a huge smile on her face.

But she didn't smile back because ... "That is so disappointing."

"What do you mean? You don't truly want to move out, do you?"

TWO

Ilia blinked at her friend, surprised by the panic in her tone. "Oh, no. I didn't mean that." She leaned forward so she could take both Korinna's and Jule's hands in hers. "Last year I felt crowded in because all of this was so new and this new body was ... well, alien to me. Plus I really just thought I was a pain in the arse to you all, complicating matters."

"I'm so sorry you felt like that," Jules said, hand turning over in Ilia's to grip tight.

"You don't feel like that now, do you?" Korinna asked.

"No! Not at all. And my feeling like that had nothing to do with you," she said, gaze moving from one to the other. "Or anyone here. You were all so welcoming and did everything you could to make me feel like this was home. No, it was more that I ..." She stopped herself, collected her thoughts. "It was fear. Fear of coming to love you all, to want to truly be a part of this family and then losing it when you all figured out I wasn't one of you."

"You *are* one of us," Korinna said, grip tightening on

Ilia's hand. "Always. Even if you'd never mated to my dad, you are family. Okay?"

Ilia nodded, blinking the tears from her eyes and swallowing down the lump in her throat.

"So, if you don't feel like that anymore, why were you disappointed that you're not causing Dawn's fits?"

She met Jule's gaze. "Because if our ... nightly activities ... were causing Dawn's nightmares and fits, then moving out would have been a solution. And ..." She shrugged. "Even though I don't want to move out, I'm disappointed that's not it. Aren't you?"

"No."

Her gaze jerked to Jules. "Why?"

"Because you both moving out would *not* have been a solution," Jules said, meeting Ilia's gaze and holding it with an emotional intensity that took Ilia's breath and made her heart pound. "As Korinna said, you're family. You belong here. With us. Okay?"

Tears threatened again and the lump that had grown in her throat made it impossible to talk, so she just nodded. She was still unused to this intensity of emotion after having spent thousands of years locked in a gem where she mostly felt numb – or raw, unfiltered fury at those who used her and abused her. This warmth of love and friendship was ... difficult. But wanted even though it still terrified her.

It was that uncomfortableness – and terror – that had her breaking the moment of soft smiles, love and camaraderie. She cleared her throat and said huskily, "I think my tea is getting cold."

"The inhumanity!" Korinna let go of Ilia's hand to pick up her mug as she said with a cheeky smile, "We wouldn't want to waste such bloody good tea!"

They all chuckled and Ilia's awkwardness slipped from her. She sipped her tea – it was actually the perfect temperature now – and took a biscuit from the tin Jules handed around.

"Yum, lemon drops. My favourite," Korinna said, putting the whole thing in her mouth.

"Please don't do that around Dawn," Jules said, looking a little horrified. "She's prone to mimicking you, and Bas and I really don't want her to learn how to do *that*."

Korinna winked as she chewed and swallowed, then after a big swig of tea to wash it down said, "The kid has to have some normalcy."

"Choking on a biscuit she's stuffed into her mouth whole isn't normal."

"But I'd teach her the art of stuffing and chewing appropriately, of course."

"Of course," Jules said, rolling her eyes. "You and Tam are going to be such bad influences."

"No. We're the best of influences. We're going to bring the fun."

"Bas and I bring the fun!"

"Yeah. But you're her parents, so it's not the same kind of fun as her brother and sister-in-law bring."

Ilia's mind flickered to her twin boys, who she'd never got to know after they were taken from her at birth and dumped in the Tyber by that bastard, Amulius. Thankfully they'd survived, but because of what had happened to her after that, the mythologies about her boys, Romulus and Remus, were the only thing she had of them. She couldn't help wondering what their lives might have been if she'd been there for them like Dawn's family was there for her. Blinking back the rawness of emotion-laden tears, she said roughly, "I think Dawn's the luckiest child in the world to have all of you."

"And you and Trip," Jules said. "If you hadn't done what you did, she wouldn't be here."

"She was only in danger because of me."

"Not true," Jules said. "You didn't tie yourself to her."

"Yeah," Korinna said. "That was entirely mine and Tam's fault when we did the spells to make you corporeal."

Jules shook her head. "No. You're both wrong to take responsibility," she said, shooting an admonishing look at both of them. "Dawn being linked to you was the influence of a higher Being. You can't deny it. She wasn't due to be born for another month and there were no signs of labour until the Void opened. It came on so quickly and the labour was over just as quickly, as if it needed to be done by a certain time." She pointed at each of them then herself as she said, "We've all been manipulated and at the mercy of wills greater than our own, so you know the feeling." Ilia and Korinna both nodded. "No, whatever is going on with Dawn, it's not any of our faults. She was born when she was, in the way she was, for a great purpose. I know this deep in my soul, but even if I didn't, the magic that's been Goddess-gifted to me is screaming that this is true."

"Your magic is telling you that?" Korinna shifted in her chair to stare at her friend and mother-in-law. "You never said this before!"

Jules looked down at her tea. "That's only because my powers are so new to me and I'm still figuring it all out, but with Bas' help and all the research I've been doing, I've come to realise that my powers react to meddling from higher Beings. And they have been unhappy for weeks."

"So, you think maybe what's going on with Dawn is causing that?"

Jules nodded at Ilia's question. "Absolutely. If the speed of her development and her extraordinarily strong powers weren't a giveaway, the fact that I feel a constant itch under my skin every time she has a fit is confirmation." Her hands gripped around her tea mug, knuckles turning white. "I don't want it to be so. I don't want her caught up in things beyond her control like we all have been. I wanted her to be free of that. But I don't think what I want for my child matters in the grand scheme of things. She wasn't born to have a normal life – I mean, she was born to a cupid with magical powers he shouldn't have and a Goddess-gifted witch after all." She chuckled, but the sound held an edge of fear. When she looked up, her eyes were swimming with tears. "I just really hope that whatever is happening, what-ever the Fates or whatever Being that's manipulating all of this has in store for us, they won't use her up. That they'll let her live. Regardless of what happens to the rest of us."

"Demeter wouldn't let anything happen to her," Ilia said, reaching out to grab Jules' hand again.

"I don't think this is Demeter. I've felt her meddling since I got my power back and this isn't that. It's more ... vast."

"Do you think it's Perses?"

She sucked in a breath. "No. This doesn't feel evil. Not that it feels good either. It just ... is."

"Then how do you know Perses isn't doing this to her?" Korinna asked.

"Because everything he's touched has been utterly evil – like Clodia." She shook her head. "No, the meddling in my daughter's life, making her be born at Easter ... it isn't him. But it's an old power. And it doesn't feel about things in the same way we do. I know she is here for a greater purpose, but I'm also afraid that she's nothing but a pawn to whatever this is that's manipulating things behind the scenes and she'll be used up and spat out at its whim."

Ilia squeezed her hand, tears welling again at the sound of utter agony in the other woman's voice. She knew too well that fear; knew too well the grief of being unable to help your own child. "She's essential. I saw it in the visions of the future Loki showed us. Whoever is responsible for what's happened to Dawn, what's happening to her, they won't let her die."

"You only saw until the coming conflict, not after it. None of us know what's coming after. We don't even truly know what's coming before or how we're supposed to face it."

"Dawn *is* essential," Korinna said softly.

"You see, Korinna agrees," Ilia said, her gaze flickering to Korinna, staying there as she noted the strange look on the ancient witch's face. "Korinna?"

"Dawn *is* essential," Korinna said again, her voice echoing in the space around them.

"Korinna? Are you okay?" Jules asked.

"Dawn *is* essential," Korinna said one more time before her eyes turned pure black. Her mug fell from her hand to smash on the floor, liquid splashing everywhere. Then she slumped in her seat.

"Korinna!" Jules dived for her as she began to slip sideways, pulling her upright before she fell off the chair.

Ilia leapt from her seat, slipping in the liquid on the floor, slamming down onto her knees, but managed to help Jules hold Korinna up just as the witch began to shudder and shake.

Then Korinna's black eyes rolled back into her head until only the whites showed.

"Tamuel," Jules yelled, her power prickling in the air

around them in a summoning spell. "Something's happening to Korinna. Come now!"

***

Whooeee! There's lots more to come for Ilia, Trip and the Stevens family in this book. I am going to put them through the wringer - as well as give you (and them) some hot, sexy times.

If you want to read more of *Fates Cursed*, you can buy your copy here:

Before you go, as promised, I have something a little extra special (and a lot sexy) for you right here. Just turn the page ...

WANT TO READ A LITTLE SOMETHING SEXY?

YOUR BONUS NSFW SCENE IS WAITING

GET YOUR EXCLUSIVE BONUS NSFW EPILOGUE TO HEARTS CURSED RIGHT HERE:

As I mentioned before, I have written a bonus NSFW sex-scene for Trip and Ilia. Ilia and Trip demanded it of me - particularly given the way the next story begins, I couldn't give them one right away there either. So, rather than let them continue to be sex-starved, I decided to sit down and write their love scene .

If you want to read it, just use the QR code or use the link below, fill in your details and it will be winging its way to you soon after.

https://www.sub-
scribepage.-
com/heartscursed_bonus_epilogue

If you've got a moment, I would love it if you could leave a review for **Hearts Cursed**. Reviews can help readers find books, and also help tell me where I'm going right and where I'm going wrong. I am grateful for all honest reviews. Thank you in advance for taking the time to let others know what you've read, and what you thought—you can leave your review at Goodreads, BookBub or the ebook retailer where you bought your copy. You can find links to the ebook retailers here:

https://www.leislleighton.com/paranormal-romance-novels/#HeartsCursed

That isn't the only special thing I've got for you. I've started serialising a hot new romantasy series exclusive to my Leisl's Legends. Turn the page to find out more …

JOIN LEISL'S LEGENDS

Subscribe to (or follow) me (via the QR code) at my Leisl's Legends page on REAM—a new subscription app like Patreon except it's designed especially for readers and authors for an amazing reading experience—and you will get early access to *The Huntress and the Vampire*  *King*, my hot enemies to lovers, witch-and-vampire-licious urban fantasy romance that readers over there are already in love with. It's the prequel novel to the first book in the Blood-Rites Series - *The Blood of the Seer*. Be the first to find out where it all began with Anita and Hei's love story.

You will also get exclusive early access to the next book

in the **Gods Cursed Series** and can comment on the story as I write it! Your feedback could be essential in shaping the next book in the series.

Be part of creating the stories you love AND get exclusive access to a whole range of goodies including other WIPs, bonus content, voting rights, signed books and much, much more.

BECOME A LEGEND NOW!
https://reamstories.com/leislleightonauthor

THE HUNTRESS AND THE VAMPIRE KING

She hates the vampire who saved her; he holds the key to her fate ...

Hunter-witch Anita Middleton wants revenge against the violent vampire cults that murdered her father and has worked hard to become one of the best vampire hunters there is. But on a difficult hunt she is caught in an ambush and is mortally wounded ... only to be saved by a mysterious warrior. A warrior with brilliant blue eyes and long silver-blonde hair who fights with a grace and violence like nothing she's seen. It is only after she wakes in the heart of his palazzo that she realises her saviour is a vampire - and according to her brother and mentor, this vampire king is their ally.

Lord Hei rules over an empire of witches, humans and vampires who have been trying to keep the vicious vampire cults, the Wild and Dark Brethren, at bay for centuries. Then he saves Anita and knows with one look she is the prophecied Huntress who could be his downfall or his salvation - and she is also his fated mate. But she struggles to trust him as her hatred of vampires is deep-seated. And she *needs* to trust him because only he can offer the specialised training a Huntress needs so her power won't overwhelm her.

But with the Dark Brethren mysteriously amassing, he has little time to win her over. And Anita must go on a crash course to learn how to control her Huntress magic ... or go slowly and violently insane.

The Huntress and the Vampire King is the exciting action-packed prequel novel to *The Blood of the Seer*.

If you love your vampires hot with a bit of The Witcher thrown in and your heroines as kick-arse as Buffy and even more tortured, if you love fated mates, enemies to lovers, chosen ones and epically hot  **romance mixed with action and mystery, then *The Huntress and the Vampire King* is what you've been waiting for.**

Sign up to Leisl's Legends (via the QR code above) and start reading exclusive early release chapters of it now!

BECOME A LEGEND NOW!
https://reamstories.com/leislleightonauthor

ALSO BY LEISL LEIGHTON

GODS CURSED SERIES

A Love Cursed Christmas Wish

Love Cursed

Soul Cursed

Blood Cursed

Hearts Cursed

Fates Cursed

Witch Cursed

Dragon Cursed

(Coming 2026)

BLOOD-RITES SERIES

The Blood of the Seer

The Blood of the Sire

The Blood of the Son

(Coming 2027)

BLOOD-RITES PREQUEL AND BONUS MATERIAL

The Huntress and the Vampire King

The Middleton Manifesto

(Available now via Leisl's Legends subscription)

~

PACK BOUND SERIES

Pack Bound

Moon Bound

Shifter Bound

Wolf Bound

Witch Bound

(A Pack Bound Series Prequel Novella)

BOX SET

Pack Bound Series Collection Books 1-4

~

DAWN OF THE CURSE

A PACK BOUND PREQUEL SERIES

Soul Bound

Alpha Bound

Hunter Bound

Fae Bound

(Coming in 2027)

ANTHOLOGIES

A Perfectly Paranormal Valentine

A Perfectly Paranormal Halloween

A Perfectly Paranormal Easter

A Perfectly Paranormal Christmas

A Perfectly Paranormal Prophecy

(Coming in 2027)

≈

As well as writing sexy, epic and romantic paranormal novels, I
write mysterious and emotional romantic suspense novels too.
Check out the following titles for amazing, suspenseful reads:

Storm Haven Series

Need You Tonight

The Devil Inside

≈

CoalCliff Stud Series

Climbing Fear: Book 1

Blazing Fear: Book 2

≈

Echo Springs Series

Dangerous Echoes: Book 1

Books 2-4 in this series, (written by Daniel deLorne, TJ Hamilton
and Shannon Curtis) are also available now at all ebook retailers.

ABOUT LEISL

Leisl Leighton is a tall red head with an overly large imagination. As a child, she identified strongly with Anne of Green Gables, and like Anne, is a voracious reader and born performer.

It came as no surprise when she went on to a career as a performer, script writer, script doctor, stage manager and musical director for cabaret and theatre restaurants.

After starting a family, Leisl stopped performing and began writing the stories plaguing her dreams. She now writes emotional stories mixed with mystery and a little bit of what goes bump in the night.

Her novels have won and placed in writing contests here and overseas. She is a passionate advocate for the romance genre, was President of Romance Writers of Australia from 2014-2017 and when she's not writing romantic stories of redemption, she is helping other authors reach their dreams with her Author Services. You can contact Leisl through her website:

www.leislleighton.com

And if you want to stay in touch and be the first to find out about new releases, appearances, special deals and exclusive content and giveaways, sign up to her Newsletter and pick up your free copy of *Fractured Curse*:

Or sign up to *Leisl's Legends* to get Fractured Curse plus serialised early access stories and bonus content:

You can also follow her on social media:

facebook.com/LeislLeightonAuthor

instagram.com/leislleightonauthor

bookbub.com/authors/leisl-leighton

amazon.com/stores/Leisl-Leighton/author/B00DBYRGZY

ACKNOWLEDGMENTS

Getting this book ready for publication was more of an adventure than I'd bargained on. In the middle of the writing process, I had a bad car accident and fractured my sternum and a vertebrae in my back and spent four days in hospital with many months of recovery ahead of me. Then just after I was able to sit up for a few hours in front of my computer and get back to my editing, my son brought Covid home and promptly gave it to my husband and me.

I felt truly sorry for myself.

But so many people, both family and friends, helped out with food packages and running errands and keeping us all going and it filled me with a sense of such love and support that despite how sick I felt, and despite the Covid coughing and sneezing kept my fracture from healing for a month—extending my healing time by another 4-6 weeks—I was able to kick myself in the butt and get up and do the work I needed to get this one finished and out in time and still have multiple rests during the day.

So huge thanks have to go to my mum and dad, Kerrie and Jim, who did so much for me during this difficult time, and to all the friends who cooked for me and sent messages of love and support. This wouldn't have happened without you.

Of course, my hubby, Mark, and my two beautiful boys, Jacob and Nathaniel, all stepped up too and when they were all feeling better, did so much to help me get back to work and took on extra duties (especially Jacob) in cooking and cleaning and washing so the house was kept in order given I wasn't able to do it.

Aside from great family and friends, a writer needs a Coven of writing peeps all their own. Thanks to my friends in my writing groups for encouraging me in this endeavour and giving me the strength to push on through all the highs and lows of doing this crazy writing thing— Laura, Chris, Marnie, Frana, Anita, Samantha and Helen. I couldn't have gotten here without you. Especially Marnie and Anita who did all the hard yards so that we could still have our retreat together even though I was recuperating from my accident and was unable to help in the ways I usually do.

Thanks once again to the insanely talented Samantha Marshall for her brilliant covers. Every day I thank the universe for bringing us together and for being able to count you friend.

Thoughts and thanks also to my bestie, Helen, and to the first writing friend I ever had, Liz. You are both gone but never forgotten and a part of you will always live on in my stories.

And a big shout out to all my friends in Romance Writers of Australia—you are inspiration and mentor rolled into a big ball of supportive writerly love. Thank you.

The final person I have to thank is my agent, Alex Adsett, for believing in me and my work and always backing every decision I make. Your confidence in me helps me believe I can actually do this writing thing. Eternal thanks.